Michael Hardwick was born in Leeds.
Before joining the Drama Department of
the BBC he was a Captain in the Indian
Army and a Film Director in New Zealand.
Since 1963 he has been a full-time freelance
author, playwright and broadcaster. Alone
or with his wife Mollie he has written
countless plays and dramatisations for radio,
television and the stage, and over sixty
books, ranging from standard literary
reference works to best-selling novels.
Most of the latter have been based on
major films and television serials including
Billy Wilder's *The Private Life of Sherlock
Holmes*, Richard Lester's *The Four
Musketeers* and John Houston's *The Man
Who Would Be King*. The Hardwicks have
been responsible for most of the *Upstairs,
Downstairs* books, Michael's share, besides
this volume, being *Mr Hudson's Diaries,
Mr Bellamy's Story*, and *Endings and
Beginnings*.

On With
The Dance

MICHAEL HARDWICK

SPHERE BOOKS LIMITED
30/32 Gray's Inn Road, London WC1X 8JL

First published in Great Britain
by Sphere Books Ltd 1975
Copyright © Sagitta Productions Ltd 1975
Reprinted 1975, 1976.

Set in Monotype Baskerville

Printed in Great Britain by
C. Nicholls & Company Ltd
The Philips Park Press, Manchester

This book is based on the first part of the fifth television series of UPSTAIRS, DOWNSTAIRS, produced by John Hawkesworth for London Weekend Television Limited, and created by Sagitta Productions Limited in association with Jean Marsh and Eileen Atkins.
Rex Firkin was the Executive Producer, and Alfred Shaughnessy was Script Editor of the series.
The author wishes to acknowledge that in writing this book he has drawn largely on material from television scripts by the following writers:

John Hawkesworth
Jeremy Paul
Alfred Shaughnessy
Rosemary Anne Sisson.

The author is grateful to them; and to London Weekend Television for the opportunity to attend recordings. He wishes to thank all connected with UPSTAIRS, DOWNSTAIRS – cast, production teams and administrators – for their co-operation and friendship.

CHAPTER ONE

EIGHT months before, the guns which had deafened Europe had been silenced, and the joyful hysteria of Armistice Day had subsided. But in July, 1919, the rejoicing still went on. In the kitchen of 165 Eaton Place the servants listened intently to the strains of the military band which accompanied the Victory March as it passed through Belgravia on its way to Buckingham Palace: right on time, twenty minutes to eleven, Mr. Hudson noted by the timetable in the newspaper. There would be soldiers, sailors, V.A.Ds., and among them their Miss Georgina in her trim uniform.

'Couldn't we slip down the end of Eaton Place and see 'em go by?' Rose ventured. 'We might just catch a glimpse of her.'

Lily, the new maid who had taken Daisy's place, backed up the head house-parlourmaid. The pleading expression on her pretty face did something to soften Mr. Hudson's heart. She had the complexion of a diarymaid, smooth shining fair hair gathered into a commendably neat knot on her slender neck, and she needed few reproofs. Mr. Hudson felt that she made an agreeable change from Daisy, who had been getting distinctly above herself since her marriage; very uppity and inclined to answer back. And Frederick, the new footman, Edward's replacement, was also a change for the better. In army life he had been Trooper Norton, Major Bellamy's soldier servant; he brought an upright demeanour, a military precision and readiness to obey orders and even anticipate them, to his job, not to mention a handsome Greek-profiled face which charmed the women.

'Be a sport, Mr. Hudson,' Rose urged, seeing the butler weakening. Mr. Hudson put up a token resistance.

'We can't have all the servants scampering out of the house at once.'

'But Miss Georgina won't be back for ages, not if she's got to march all the way down through the East End and fetch up again at Hyde Park Corner this afternoon.'

'What if the Major comes in?' said Mrs. Bridges, the cook.

'He won't be back till after twelve o'clock at least.'

'How do you know?'

'The Major,' said Mr. Hudson with pride, 'is on duty at the Saluting Base opposite Buckingham Palace, escorting important personages to their seats.'

'Well, then,' Mrs. Bridges pleaded, 'let 'em go out and see what they can. It's not every day we have a procession come by here.'

Mr. Hudson gave in. 'Oh, very well, just down to the corner of Belgrave Street and no further, mind. And behave yourselves. No pushing or shouting on the pavement.'

He watched them go; the sedate Rose, the eager Lily, Ruby with flour on her hands and her hair on end. Then, armed with his father's old deer-stalking telescope, he led Mrs. Bridges upstairs to the drawing-room balcony, from which they could see clearly the marching figures, the stiff-backed generals on their horses, the glitter of bayonets and swords in the July sun, the Naval Detachment immaculately shipshape and Bristol-fashion, the red, white and blue of the nurses.

Standing there, the music, cheering and tramping in their ears, both felt thankful for a lively interlude in a world which had become strangely drab. Hazel Bellamy was dead, a victim of the terrible influenza which had swept the country last year. The Major had taken his wife's death badly: but then he took everything badly. Lonely, neurotic, inward-turned, he spent most of his time shut up in his room, where he could be heard playing noisy ragtime music on his gramophone. Sometimes Miss Georgina would sit with him, but more often she was out at parties and dances. Mr. Hudson shook his head at the thought. Once the staff had suspected that there was 'something between' the Major and Miss Georgina. After all, they were suited in age, and there was no actual

8

relationship. But since the excitement of the war had died down, whatever spark they had lit in each other had died down with it. No. 165 had become a sad, dust-sheeted house.

Lord Bellamy had made a wonderful new start, of course, with his marriage to the pretty, sparkling widow who had been Virginia Hamilton. Curious to think of him and her and her two children in a house of their own, which they were hoping to buy when they returned from Paris. Mr. Hudson felt they would leave a gap in his life.

It was late afternoon when Georgina and James returned. Georgina collapsed on the stairs and dragged off her shoes. 'Thank God *that's* over,' she said. 'My feet are bloody well killing me.'

'Georgina!' James was shocked. Even now that women were emancipated and their skirts were getting shorter and shorter, it seemed strange and wrong to hear them swear.

'Well, they are. One of the Queen Alexandras behind us said she'd read in the paper it was over five miles.'

'Good for you. Keep you slim.'

'It's all very well for you, sitting down in a covered stand all the time.'

'I didn't sit down all day. Had to keep giving out free souvenir programmes to all the high-ups, including an Indian Prince who handed me five pounds.'

She laughed. 'Did you give it back?'

'Had to, unfortunately.'

Mr. Hudson appeared, genie-like, to express his approbation. 'Mrs. Bridges and I managed to see something of the procession from the drawing-room balcony, and I understand Rose and the others caught a wee glimpse of you in the V.A.D.'s column. They were very proud and excited, Miss.'

'There you are,' James said. 'Wasn't it worth sore feet?'

Mr. Hudson watched them go upstairs together, the tall slender uniformed man, with the limp which would never leave him, and the pretty girl in her trim uniform. His

9

face was sad and brooding as he went downstairs to the servants' hall.

'Tea's ready, Mr. Hudson,' Rose announced. 'And you'll never guess who's come to see us.'

'I've no idea.'

'You go in and see for yourself.'

What Mr. Hudson saw for himself, seated at the tea-table with Mrs. Bridges pouring tea for them, was Edward and Daisy. It was hard to believe they had ever been part of the household. Edward's civilian suit fitted him considerably worse than his footman's uniform had done. His military moustache had gone, leaving a look of bareness behind it, and his hair shone with violet-scented brilliantine. Daisy wore a large, ostentatious hat, and her unbecoming high-waisted dress emphasised the fact that she was some months pregnant.

Mrs. Bridges beamed. 'They come in for a cup of tea and to see how we all was.'

'That's right,' said Edward. Daisy bestowed on Mr. Hudson a superior smile.

'You haven't changed a scrap, Mr. Hudson. Has he, Eddie?'

'No, but I have.' Edward sleeked down his hair. 'I'm a civvy, now, you see. What they call a door-to-door sales-man.'

'He goes round from house to house,' Rose explained, 'ringing the bell and selling people hairbrushes, bootlaces and combs and that, out of a suitcase.'

'I see.' Mr. Hudson did not appear impressed.

'Only temporary, mind,' Daisy put in hastily, seeing his expression. 'He's . . . he's thinking of chucking it in and getting a more permanent situation as storeman in a furniture place out Romford way.'

'So we can settle down in a nice house, out of London,' Edward amplified. 'And Daisy can have the baby, where there's a bit of garden.'

'Daisy's expecting Christmas time,' Mrs. Bridges explained.

'So I observe,' Mr. Hudson said coldly. 'Congratulations, both of you.'

Daisy bridled proudly. She was thoroughly enjoying herself, the only married woman present, a Little Stranger on the way, a husband who was no longer the slave of Mr. Hudson or anybody else; only nobody seemed as impressed as she had hoped they'd be. Lily entered, and Daisy looked without pleasure on the girl who had taken her place, and who was undoubtedly as pretty as a picture. Edward was equally daunted by the handsome appearance and soldierly carriage of Frederick, when his successor joined them for tea. Somehow, they'd both thought they were irreplaceable; but nobody seemed to feel the draught.

Cheekily, Edward asked, 'Well, how's the nobs, then – all flourishing?'

'The nobs?' Mr. Hudson repeated the term in a voice of awful chill.

'I think Edward's referring to the Family upstairs,' Rose explained unnecessarily.

'Then he should say so,' returned Mr. Hudson, and went on, fixing Edward with a steely eye. 'For your information, Edward, the Major and Miss Georgina are in residence here and both "flourishing", as you put it. His Lordship and Lady Bellamy went over to Versailles for the signing of the Peace Treaty and remained in Paris for their honeymoon.'

Edward stared. 'What, all you lot to wait on the Major and Miss Georgina?'

'I shouldn't fancy you've got enough to do, have you?' Daisy added.

This was so painfully true that Mr. Hudson was goaded into rising abruptly.

'Frederick,' he said. 'If you can spare a moment.'

Frederick had only just started his tea, but obedience was second nature to him. 'Yes, Mr. Hudson,' he said, swallowing his first mouthful of bread and butter.

'I should like to go through the cellar book with you and check the port wine. There are a number of bottles to be earmarked for His Lordship. If you would kindly come with me to the pantry . . .'

'Certainly, Mr. Hudson.'

'I shall be making you responsible from now on for checking and ordering the spirits and minerals,' Mr. Hudson told him as they vanished cellarwards, making Edward feel smaller than ever, for he had never been awarded such a responsibility. Rose, Lily and Ruby gazed fondly after Frederick's straight back. 'Lily and me think he's quite good-looking, don't we, Lil?' Rose said.

Daisy was furious. It was all a plot to disparage Eddie and herself. Edward covertly glanced at her flushed face.

'Well,' he said brightly, 'me and Dais mustn't stop too long. We're thinking of taking a walk through Hyde Park, see all the dancing and singing, and there's fireworks later.'

'You people going out to see the fireworks?' Daisy enquired patronisingly.

'Not tonight,' said Rose.

'And we're not "people" neither, Daisy.' Mrs. Bridges' voice and look were enough to cool the well-cosied teapot. Silently, Edward and Daisy prepared for departure. They were not wanted any more.

Taking a tray of whisky and soda into James's room that evening, Frederick thought that peace seemed to be doing the Major no good. Slumped in a chair, a pipe in his mouth, he looked the picture of bored melancholy. Georgina, lying on a sofa in a Japanese-patterned teagown, flipping through the *Tatler* magazine, gave Frederick a pretty smile. Once it would have been thrilling for her to be alone with James like this. Now, somehow, the excitement had gone out of it. At least the ex-Trooper Norton was someone to flirt with.

'Little did I realise,' said James, taking the glass Frederick had poured for him, 'when you used to bring me that revolting stew in a mess-tin down in the dugout with the shells bursting outside, that one day you'd be handing me a whisky and soda in my own house. I'll bet you never did, either.'

'It did occur to me as a possibility, sir,' Frederick replied, gazing straight before him as a footman should. 'When I came here with your kit, sir, after you were posted missing.'

James stared. 'How could it? Everyone thought I was dead.'

'I didn't, sir.'

'He had faith – didn't you, Frederick?' Georgina said.

As Frederick began to agree a sudden burst of sound shocked James almost out of his chair. 'What the devil's that row?'

'That'll be the fireworks in Hyde Park, sir.'

Georgina ran to the window and opened it, staring with wide wondering eyes at the flashes of gold and green, the showers of glittering sparks, the tails of white fire bursting in the air with resounding bangs. 'Oh, look! There! Oh, how lovely, all red and orange!'

The bangs and cracks were going through James's head. 'Thank you, Frederick,' he said, 'that's all,' anxious to get the footman out of the room before he began to shake visibly. But Georgina was still intent on the fiery spectacle.

'Do come and look, Jumbo. Such marvellous colours, and you can see everything . . .'

James had his hands over his ears. 'Close the window, Georgina.'

She turned, surprised. 'Why?'

'Because . . .' he looked round the room for inspiration, 'because I want you to hear a new record I bought at Selfridge's. It's the latest jazz-band – playing rather a jolly tune.' He was putting on the record, winding the handle, anything to stop himself wincing and shuddering at the explosions. Only when the saxophones of 'The Darktown Strutters' Ball' almost drowned them did Georgina turn away from the window and see his distress. She shut the window and came over to him, taking him in her arms.

'There, Jumbo, it's all right. It's all right.'

Mrs. Bridges and Mr. Hudson were at a loose end. It was only mid-morning, yet the housework was done, finished by Lily and Rose in a quarter of the time it would once have taken. Frederick, having completed his duties, had been given an hour off, and Ruby dispatched to the butcher's. Both the older servants were thinking of the same thing.

'Of course,' said Mrs. Bridges, 'she'll have to have a proper staff, wherever it is they're going to live. I mean, His Lordship's been accustomed to having servants wait on him, ever since he married Lady Marjorie. He wouldn't like having to fend for himself.'

Mr. Hudson sighed. 'It's a question of money, Mrs. Bridges. Wages are a good deal higher nowadays, and Her Ladyship's not wealthy. And it'll be a smaller house than this one – with a modest household.'

Mrs. Bridges looked shocked. 'You mean, just a cook-general and one girl to do all the rest, like the middle-class families have out in the suburbs?'

'I wouldn't be surprised.'

It was her turn to sigh. 'Well, I don't know, I'm sure. Perhaps it's time you and me give up service and retired.'

'The thought has crossed my mind more than once since the end of the war,' he said.

'I mean, from what you say, they're not likely to take us on in their new house, any of us. The Major and Miss Georgina can look after themselves now. And I'm not staring work in a new place at my age . . .'

The shrilling of the telephone in the passage interrupted their gloomy reflections. Mr. Hudson's face brightened as he answered it and heard Richard Bellamy's voice at the other end. After a short conversation he returned to report to Mrs. Bridges.

'They're back from Paris, safe and sound.'

'Staying at the Hyde Park hotel again?'

'Aye, but his lordship wants two or three of his suits, his cigar-case, and a few other items he left behind here. He's coming over to fetch them at tea-time.'

'I see. How did he sound?'

'Remarkably cheerful. And who's to blame him?'

Later that afternoon James rose from his armchair to greet his father. Richard waved him down.

'Don't get up, old boy.' He bestowed an affectionate pat on the shoulder as James subsided again, and took another chair himself. James could sense a new briskness and relaxation in his father's manner. Richard gave him his characteristically tentative smile, using only one side of his mouth. The greyness which had conquered the dark of his hair enhanced his good looks, and, with his slim figure, belied his age, rather than accentuating it.

'Everything all right?'

'I suppose so.' The smile faded at James's morose tone. If, in his new contentment, Richard had hoped to find a corresponding change in his son, he was disappointed.

'Did you enjoy Paris?' James made the effort to ask.

'Fascinating. Versailles was like one great international garden party . . .'

He would have gone on, but it was patently obvious that James had enquired merely as a rudimentary courtesy. Richard finished lamely, 'I just came round to fetch a few things. Hudson's packing a valise for me. With . . . your permission, I trust?'

'*My* permission?'

'He's your butler, James.'

'And yours, Father.'

Richard shook his head. 'I no longer live here.'

An awkward silence fell between them, broken at length by Richard.

'Do you prefer to sit up here – in your room? I mean, the life of this house has always centred on the morning-room.'

'The morning-room depresses me. Besides, I prefer my own company to other people's these days. I'm happy enough up here, with my books and things.'

Richard frowned his concern. 'I should have thought it more depressing to shut yourself up. You know, you must try to cheer up, old boy.'

'It's not easy, Father.'

'I know.'

15

'The house is so quiet. Even the servants haven't enough to do. But I can't give them notice, after all these years, or I'd seriously think of selling the house. Then, where would Georgina go? She has no other home, until she marries. Besides, I want to live here. It's my home.'

Richard nodded, infected now by his son's depression. James said, 'You and Virginia – have you found a place yet?'

'A house?' Richard attempted nonchalance, but failed. 'Oh, Virginia's seen one or two she likes, but nothing's settled. It takes time, you know.'

The intensity of passion with which James responded startled Richard.

'Live here, Father. Please! This house can be yours again, from top to bottom. Just leave me my two rooms and Georgina hers. I can't run it alone, and it'd save you having to get something else. Please, Father.'

Richard felt his growing gloom replaced by pity for his son, a victim, it seemed to him, of life and circumstances and of something unenviable in his very genes; almost, it occurred to him, that same black vein of self-destruction that had made his own brother, Arthur Bellamy, his own worst enemy and blighted his life and others' in their turn.

He said, 'It's a very kind offer, old boy, and I'm very touched. I'm sure Virginia would be too. Only . . .'

'What?'

'It would have to be her decision. She is my wife and will be mistress of whatever house we choose to live in. As you know, she's pretty sure of what she wants in life – not someone to be easily talked out of anything, once her mind's made up.'

'But if you haven't actually bought a house yet, surely . . .'

'Yes, yes. I'll speak to her about it, of course. This evening. But don't hang too much hope on it, James. You must remember that recently married people . . . well, usually prefer some degree of privacy.'

His new sympathy for his son decreased abruptly when he heard the bitter retort, 'Privacy? With two noisy children shouting all over the house! Look, Father, don't even bother to ask her. 'You're not in favour of it yourself, I can see, so just let's forget it.'

Restraining himself from replying in kind, Richard said, mixing firmness with genuine sympathy: 'I don't know what's the matter with you, James. I do know – we all know – that you've had a rotten deal, with the war and then losing Hazel. But one has to go forward in life, build something new, find something worthwhile to do. You're alive, you've got enough money to live on in sufficient comfort.' He got up. 'Don't give up, old boy. I shall speak to Virginia tonight. I promise.'

James roused himself to nod his thanks.

'Do your best, Father.'

Richard nodded, all too aware what Virginia's likeliest answer would be.

'I will. Now I'd better see if Hudson's got my case ready. Give our love to Georgina, will you? – Virginia's and mine.'

'Yes. She'll be in . . . sometime, I suppose.'

He lapsed into his increasing habit of staring unseeing into space. After a moment's hesitation Richard left the room. James did not hear him go.

Mr. Hudson was in the hall, trying to appear busy, when Richard came down. Richard's packed case stood near the front door.

'May I call you a taxi, m'lord?' the butler asked.

'Thank you, Hudson.'

'Er, will you be sending over for the remainder of your belongings? I can instruct Frederick to have them packed and ready.'

Richard considered. 'I think . . . until her ladyship settles on a house my things might as well stay here.'

It was not the decisive reply, one way or another, that Mr. Hudson had been seeking, but it would have to suffice.

'I shall go and sit in the morning-room while you telephone for the taxi,' Richard told him.

'I, er, am not sure whether Rose has raised the blinds yet

or aired the room, m'lord. I'm afraid since the Major comes downstairs so rarely these days, and Miss Georgina . . . is so often out . . .' He ventured a desperate try. 'No doubt the Major will be closing down the house altogether in due course . . . er . . . er . . .' He wanted to add 'and dispensing with a staff', but couldn't bring himself to ask so direct a question of the former master whom he had served for so many years.

Aware of the anxiety, which it occurred to him for the first time must be prevalent below stairs, Richard could only answer, 'Things are far from settled, I'm afraid, Hudson. Don't ask me what the future holds.'

He let himself into the morning-room. The confident briskness with which he had come to his old home that afternoon was altogether gone now.

When he returned to No. 165 two days later he had Virginia on his arm. She appeared, to Mr. Hudson, opening the door to them, younger than before. He had always thought her too apparently young to have lost a son in action; now it seemed even less credible. In her ivory-coloured dress and matching light coat and her fetching 'Merry Widow' hat she gave an impression of light, immediately dispelling the gloom of the silent house. Hudson's spirits rose a little. If only . . .

'Welcome home, my lady,' he beamed. 'The Major had to go out briefly, my lord. He gave orders for you to be shown into the drawing-room until lunchtime. Rose has opened up one end, and I have put a decanter of sherry in there.'

'I've never seen your drawing-room,' Virginia reminded Richard as they went upstairs.

'James's,' he corrected her.

The drawing-room was for the most part dust-sheeted, a repository for scarcely identifiable lumpy shapes, with the pictures covered and most of the blinds drawn. Richard wrinkled his nose at the mustiness as he went to raise another blind, admitting more of the cheering sunshine.

'Like a furniture store,' he grumbled.

'It's beautiful,' Virginia said.

'Well, it's seen some interesting gatherings in its time.'

'I'm sure the whole house is full of memories for you, darling. I think that's partly why I'm so anxious for us to have our own place.'

Richard went to pour sherry from the decanter on the closed grand piano, thinking unhappily of the forthcoming interview with James. She went on, 'That little house in Clarendon Street would be perfect for us. I could make it so comfortable and charming.'

He said diffidently, 'There's room for all of us here,' and added quickly, 'for the time being'; but she was shaking her head emphatically.

'No, Richard. I know we've been asked here to lunch because James wants to persuade me, and hopes you'll support him. It puts me in a very awkward postion. What am I to say to him? You know I don't want to come and live here. It's not my home, and it's not yours any more. So please . . .'

She was interrupted by James's entrance. Richard could see immediately that he was on his best behaviour, smiling and businesslike as he limped energetically down the big room to them.

'I'm awfully sorry. Good morning, Virginia. 'Morning, Father. I had to go out to the bank.'

'I was just admiring your lovely drawing-room,' Virginia smiled. 'Such elegance. And that ceiling !'

'Yes. Splendid, isn't it ? I thought we'd use it, for a change. Sort of celebrate your return. Ah, I see Hudson's used his initiative.'

'We helped ourselves,' Richard said, handing his son a filled glass.

'Good. Well, then . . . here's to your return . . . to Eaton Place.'

A silence continued after they had drunk, until Richard said, 'Virginia and I have seen a rather fine little house just north of Hyde Park.'

'In Clarendon Street,' Virginia added. 'Just about perfect for us, and a price we can afford.'

James looked into his glass. 'Did you happen to mention to Virginia what I said the other day, Father?'

Before his father could reply, Virginia had said, in a tone so gentle that she might have been addressing one of her own children, rather than a man a year or two her senior, 'James, come and sit beside me and let me try to explain.'

And as petulantly as a child he answered, 'There's no point.' But he obeyed, and they took places side by side on the settee. Richard joined them.

'I do understand how you feel,' she told James earnestly. 'I know it's very sad and quiet for you, all alone in this house. Perhaps you'll want to sell it eventually and find some comfortable rooms somewhere.'

James stirred restlessly. 'Where would Georgina go? This is her home, as well as mine. And the responsibility for her is mine now, no longer my father's.'

'I understand that, too.'

'And the servants? If I leave here they'll all have to be given notice. All of them. It's unthinkable.'

'I know, James, I know.' Virginia was fighting herself now, as well as him; trying not to weaken. 'You must see this from my point of view, too. I've married your father, whom I dearly love, and we're looking forward to a fresh start, away from our own sad memories. I have my two children to consider. I want them to grow up in a home that's theirs, not someone else's. You and your father have been through so much in this house, James; sad times and happy times as well. I think those memories, and the house itself, will belong to you both for ever, but in the past. The war's over now, and I think we all hope you can find a new life and a new kind of happiness. So, please allow your father to find his new happiness and his new life, too.'

James did not need to exaggerate, even unconsciously, the depth of his self-pity.

'I can't argue with what you say. The idea that you

20

should come and live here was just a thought – a silly thought. My greatest wish is for you and Father to be happy. I'm sure that before too long Georgina will marry and have a home of her own. Meanwhile, it's just that . . . well, six people to wait on . . . one tiresome, bad-tempered widower . . .'

He bit off the rest of his sentence as one of those six people entered the room. 'Luncheon is served, sir,' Mr. Hudson told him.

James heaved himself to his feet and straightened his back. 'Come along, Virginia,' he said, offering his arm. 'I want to hear all about Versailles and your stay in Paris.'

As they filed past him, Hudson, beside the door, searched each profile, but still nothing gave him the answer he and his fellow servants awaited.

It came a few days later. At James's order, Mr. Hudson had mustered the staff into a line in the servants' hall. James came limping down the stairs, his great height causing him to stoop to safeguard his head. He nodded to them. 'Do sit down, Mrs. Bridges, please.' She thanked him and resumed the chair from which she had risen. James cleared his throat and addressed them in tones he had often used at the Front, a blend of decision and compassionate understanding.

'I expect you can all guess why I've asked you to see me this morning. I'm afraid this is a very sad occasion for me, because, as you may have heard, my father and stepmother are going to live in a house of their own and . . . and since Mrs. Bellamy's death I haven't felt able to justify living by myself in so large a house as this with . . . with a full staff, you see . . .' He swallowed and plunged on, less confidently now. 'So I'm afraid the . . . the sad moment has come for me to say thanks to you all for the years of devoted service – well, anyway, those of you who've been with us since before the war – and ask you to consider yourselves under a month's notice . . . I mean, to have time to find positions in other households. I'm really and truly sorry that such a time has come, but I must now think of selling the house and moving into rooms, so in any case I can't possibly keep a staff on any longer. I can only repeat my grateful thanks to you all.'

He had never felt so wretched, even about sending men over the top in hopeless circumstances. The faces in front of him showed, in varying degrees, regret, unhappiness, apprehension, and even fear of the unknown future. The example of Edward and Daisy had not been overlooked.

Mr. Hudson spoke up in the way it had been agreed he should if ever this present situation were to come about.

'If I might be permitted, sir, to speak on behalf of us all, we had anticipated such an eventuality as this, and please be assured that we understand your difficult position. Sir, I am authorised to say that all of us below stairs are willing to continue in your service for reduced wages, if that could in any way influence you to change your mind.'

James answered, 'It's very good of you Hudson – of all of you – and naturally I'm very touched by your offer. But it's not really a question of wages. It's just that this house is too big for me alone, and Miss Georgina and I . . . well, I'm afraid we've reached the end of a chapter. That . . . that's all I can say. Thank you.'

He almost fled back up the stairs, leaving them motionless, stunned by the shock that was none the less for having been half expected. Mr. Hudson rallied them in the best way he knew. 'Very well. About your duties now, all of you.'

Mrs. Bridges got to her feet. 'Come along, Ruby, and help me with the vegetables.'

Rose moved out of the line-up like an automaton. 'After all them years !' she said to the air.

'You'll find another place easy enough, Rose,' Mrs. Bridges assured her. 'You're young enough and healthy. And so will Lily and Frederick. I'm not so sure about you, Ruby,' she added, meaning it as a heavy joke rather than an unkindness, which the girl was too unsubtle to recognise. She retorted, 'I'll get work in a hotel, easy. I've seen advertisements in t'newspapers for kitchen staff for hotels and boarding houses. And they pay good money, nowadays.'

Mrs. Bridges snorted and they went off into the kitchen together. Lily and Frederick had gone. Only Mr. Hudson and Rose remained. He seated himself dejectedly at the plain table and she went to take a chair opposite him.

'I expect you'll be thinking of retirement now, Mr. Hudson. That is, if you've got enough saved.'

He shook his head, but there was little determination in his eyes.

'I hadn't anticipated giving up service yet awhile, Rose.'

'No, but if it's a question of finding a little house somewhere and putting some money down, I mean, there's always what my Gregory left me in the bank. I could . . . let you have some of that, if it would help.'

Only later did he see the irony in this gesture from the spinster who, on several dramatic occasions, had accused him of blighting her hopes, conniving with Fate to keep her unmarried and in service, of having a perpetual 'down' on her. He patted her hand and smiled wearily. 'It's a very kind thought, Rose, and much appreciated. But you'll need all your savings for yourself. In old age a woman can become needy sooner than a man. As long as I am blessed with good health I shall continue in service as a butler, provided a suitable place can be found. Otherwise, perhaps, as porter at a club or one of those new apartment houses.'

She was not really listening. 'All good things have to come to an end, don't they? We've had a good run.'

'Aye. The very words Mrs. Bridges used the other day.'

Rose got up with a sigh. 'Well, there's still the laundry to be sorted out.'

She went, leaving him sitting, unable to issue himself with any orders which would occupy his hands or his mind.

James told Georgina what had happened when she came in from having a lesson in dancing the Fox-Trot and the Black Bottom. She took the implications for her own future with the easygoing indifference of the well-attached Society girl, but worried about James, depressed and haunted by the expressions he had seen on those faces in

23

the servants' hall. He told her about the ordeal of breaking the news.

'Oh, how awfully weepy!' she exclaimed, sincere despite the slang. 'I wish you hadn't told me that. Anyway, I think they've been happy here. It's been like home to them for such a long time, hasn't it?'

'That makes it worse,' James said grimly.

'I'm sorry, Jumbo. Try not to think about it. Tell me some news. I haven't seen you since Wednesday.'

'There isn't much. I had a letter from Father. They're bringing the children to London on Friday for a few days. William's got the dentist and Alice needs some new clothes.'

'I'm longing to see the children. Why not invite them to tea?'

'Are you suggesting I entertain a couple of brats while Father and Virginia go off shopping?'

'Yes, I am – only I'd be here to help you. I adore children.'

'Oh, well, if you're going to take part . . . Only, mind you do.'

And she did, as did every member of the staff, save only Mr. Hudson, whose role was confined to hovering uncertainly, apprehensive for the sound of something fragile being shattered or the report of one of their small guests having been sick on an immaculate carpet. Neither fear was realised. Georgina and the servants liked Alice and William on sight, and, after a brief period of natural awe on the part of children unused to so grand a house or so many servants, found themselves evidently liked in return. As the pretty Alice and the lively William gained confidence, the pace of their exploration quickened, and so did their consumption of food and drink. After they had demolished a quantity of paste sandwiches, jelly, specially baked cake and lemonade which Mrs. Bridges had envisaged having to be finished off for them by the servants that evening, there was no hesitation about the way in which they answered Georgina's inquiry whether they had had enough, and Lily had to be despatched to the kitchen for more supplies.

'Poor mites!' Mrs. Bridges declared. 'That's what comes of living in hotels. Ruby, fetch out the shrimp paste again and cut some more bread.'

Mr. Hudson winced as the whistle of the speaking tube sounded shrilly outside. He had answered it three times already, and each time heard only childish giggles at the other end.

'Little devils,' said Mrs. Bridges, smiling when Mr. Hudson returned to report that this time someone had blown down into his ear. 'What time are his lordship and her ladyship fetching them, Mr. Hudson?'

'About half-past six.' He smiled rather forcedly: he would not have smiled at all if he had known that it was Rose upstairs who had shown Master William how the tube worked and urged him to try it in the first place.

'Would you listen to the wee rascals?' he exclaimed as the sound of heavy pounding of piano keys reached their ears.

'Bless my soul!' Mrs. Bridges beamed. 'That piano hasn't been played for donkey's years. Not since Miss Lizzie left home.'

The 'tune' was 'Chopsticks', and this time Georgina was the instigator, playing the treble to Alice's obedient bass. When William heard them he ran to the drawing-room and, of course, demanded to join in, so a third pair of hands was added to the performance, and a third voice pealing with delighted laughter.

James, who had done his best to look and sound benevolent, but had been relieved to leave Georgina, Rose and Frederick to participate most actively in the afternoon's entertaining, warily entered the drawing-room to show willing.

'Sorry, James,' Georgina shouted above the din. 'Is it too much for you? We'll stop, if you like.'

'It's all right,' he bellowed back, though his head was beginning to hammer slightly. Then inspiration came to him. He called, 'I wondered whether William would care to come up and see my train?'

The playing halted. Georgina asked the flushed little boy, 'Would you, William?'

'A train! Oh, yes please!'

'Come along, then,' James said, and tentatively took the child's hand to lead him away. Georgina, Alice and Rose followed.

When Mr. Hudson let Richard and Virginia in, Richard enquired uncertainly, 'Everything all right, Hudson?'

'Oh, yes, my lord,' the butler was able to say truthfully. If he had had his own reservations at first, none of the others had; and the sound of sustained gaiety in the house which had for so long been shadowed by doleful quiet had quite lifted his spirits.

'Yes, m'lord,' he said again. 'Things have been quite lively in the house.'

'I'm so glad,' Virginia said. 'But I must round them up and take them away before they wreck the house.'

'Let's go up,' Richard grinned, 'and assess the damage.'

When they reached the open nursery door they paused at the threshold and stared. On the floor knelt James, in the act of restoring a toppled clockwork locomotive to its track for William to start off again. Behind them, Rose had the front of the dolls' house open and was showing Alice items from the miniature tea-set. Nearby, Georgina was squatting on the floor, trying to dress a doll.

As Richard and Virginia looked at one another James glanced up and saw them.

'Hello, Virginia – Father,' he said, in a tone more cheerful than they had heard for they didn't know how long. 'I say, these wretched points are sticking. Need a drop of oil.'

Feeling as if she were including him in the order, Virginia said, 'Come along now, children. I'm afraid it's time to go.'

The children protested in unison, but their mother shook her head. 'It's gone half-past six. Come along downstairs and get your coats on.' But Rose was already going. 'I'll fetch them, m'lady.'

Georgina struggled to her feet. 'Alice and I have been playing the piano together, haven't we? Rather well, we thought.'

'And blowing through the whistle,' Alice added excitedly. 'Oh, Mummy, it's a such a lovely house. You can talk through the whistle to someone in the basement all the way from upstairs.'

William put in, 'And there's lots of rooms to hide in, and cupboards for hide and seek.'

'Yes, I . . . I'm sure there are,' Virginia faltered. 'But you must say goodbye now and come downstairs. We mustn't outstay our welcome.'

James, standing beside her now, murmured, 'That would be quite impossible, Virginia, and you know it.'

'Couldn't they stay for just another half hour?' Georgina pleaded, a child again herself. 'Please, Virginia.'

Cornered and out-gunned, Virginia heard Richard say, 'Why not let them, darling? If they're having fun.'

All eyes were on her face. Everyone was hanging on her decision. She had no option left.

'Very well. But just for half an hour.'

James was already discussing the sticking points with William and Georgina had sunk down to take up the doll again as Richard and Virginia turned away towards the stairs.

When the half hour, and a little more, was up, James and Georgina dutifully came into the drawing-room, where Virginia had been playing the piano to Richard a good deal more softly and expertly than it had been played earlier.

'Rose is getting their coats on,' Georgina said. 'Hudson's calling a taxi.'

Rose appeared at the door at that moment, the children behind her. 'Beg pardon, m'lady, but we're just going down to say thank you to Mrs. Bridges for our tea.'

27

Virginia stepped forward. 'I'd like to take them down to the kitchen myself. May I?' she asked James.

'Of course.'

Mrs. Bridges looked up with surprise from her mixing bowl and hastily wiped her floury fingers on her apron.

'The children just wanted to come down and say goodbye, and thank you for their tea,' Virginia told her.

'Oh, it was a pleasure, my lady, I'm sure.'

'This is William – and Alice.'

'How do you do, my dears? Did you have enough to eat?'

'Oh, yes, thank you. It was a lovely tea.'

'Especially the jelly.'

Mrs. Bridges beamed. 'Well, next time Mummy brings you here to tea I'll make some nice strawberry tarts, eh? How about that?' Impulsively, she seized the children in turn and gave them a great hug. Virginia felt tears start behind her eyes. With further thanks to Mrs. Bridges she hustled them back up to the hall, where Mr. Hudson hovered as usual.

'His lordship is up in the drawing-room, m'lady. Your taxi should be here in two or three minutes.'

She thanked him and took the children up to the drawing-room, where she found Richard wih James and Georgina. The gravity of her husband's expression surprised and alarmed her, and she was glad that the children ran down the big room out of immediate earshot.

'What's the matter?' she asked, low.

'D'you know what James has just told me?' Richard said. 'All the servants are under month's notice.'

James appealed to her. 'What else could I do? I can't go on living here.'

Virginia did not respond at once, but then said slowly, almost to herself, 'Rose seems to have a wonderful way with children. Better than my old nanny.'

'She'd make a marvellous children's maid,' Georgina agreed.

'Who'd do the housework?' Virginia speculated.

'Lily. We only need one housemaid now, don't we, James?'

Hardly daring to, James muttered agreement. Georgina said, 'Frederick would valet Uncle Richard, as well as you, James. And Lily's such a good housemaid that Rose would have time to be Virginia's lady's maid as well . . . That is . . . I mean, if . . .'

Georgina checked herself, embarrassed.

'Does there really have to be an "if"?' James asked huskily.

He could have cursed Hudson for choosing that moment to enter and announce, 'The taxi is here, m'lady.'

'Thank you, Hudson,' Virginia said serenely, summoning the children with a wave. 'And thank you, Georgina and James, for looking after these two for me. They've had a lovely time and you've really spoiled them.'

'That's all right,' Georgina answered, subdued now.

Virginia smiled at Richard. 'I think we'd better telephone the agents tomorrow morning and withdraw our offer for the house in Clarendon Street. Don't you?'

He floundered: 'You don't mean . . . Are you sure, Virginia? I mean . . . Please . . . !'

Her smile embraced them all. 'Yes, I do mean. I may be a pretty stubborn and obstinate person, Richard, but I know when I'm beaten. Come along, children.'

And without a backward look she shooed children and husband away before her.

CHAPTER TWO

WITHIN minutes of Virginia's decision the news of their reprieve had been given to the staff. James delivered it himself, feeling it the least he could do after having pronounced sentence in the first place. Only subconsciously was he prompted by the certainty that a *fait accompli* in this quarter would disarm his stepmother of any possibility of changing her mind.

Richard and Virginia's move into his former home was managed, with almost imperceptible smoothness, by an eager and now happy Mr. Hudson. Apart from new faces above and below stairs, and some modernisation of the decor of certain parts of the house, the only substantial difference lay in the exuberant presence of two young children. Long years before, of course there had been a boy child and a girl – James and Elizabeth – compared with whom William and Alice seemed to Hudson to be allowed a wee bit too much licence to come and go as they pleased. But if this were to be all the change that had to be borne, it was small indeed alongside the post-war upheaval Mr. Hudson had foreseen, and he was content to bear with it.

Barely had she heard with equal relief that she was to be kept on than Rose received a letter from Southwold, where she had been born the daughter of the gatekeeper to the estate of the late Earl of Southwold, Richard Bellamy's father-in-law. It was to tell her that her aunt there had died and to ask her to attend the funeral and help sort out some neglected and complicated affairs. She was reluctant to ask for extended leave at such a moment, but Virginia insisted on her staying for quite as long as might prove necessary.

'I won't say you're not indispensable here, Rose,' she smiled, 'but I'm sure we'll manage while you're away.'

Only Lily grumbled about the extra burden of work

she would have to carry, but found the taste of brief superiority to her liking. In the way that upset or gloom upstairs had always had its way of depressing the spirits of those below, a general air of contentment about the household as a whole subtly touched everyone alike. Even James, at this time, cast aside his lethargy and infectious gloom. His personal future was still so vague as to seem non-existent; but his immediate dilemma had been solved in the way he had wanted it to be, and even he had grace enough to show his thanks through the nearest he could rise to cheerfulness.

He roused himself into going about more, becoming an almost daily visitor to his club, the Guards'. It was there one morning that he heard something from a fellow-member which, though he would at one time probably have brushed it aside with some cynical comment, caused him to sit down and dash off a letter, which he sent out immediately to the post. He re-read it the following morning, in print, in *The Times*. Mr. Hudson read it, too, aloud and with pride to the servants. Richard Bellamy read it, and so did many others. Its burden was this:

'I have recently heard of a story which fills me with horror, dismay and shame. It is the case of a former sergeant of the King's Royal Rifle Corps, unable to find employment, who has been reduced to living for the past nine months, with his wife and four children, in a patch-work shack made up of tarpaulins and old army ground-sheets. The total space in which the family must live, eat and sleep is ten feet by six.

'Nor is this an isolated incident. I am informed that there are thousands of ex-Servicemen of all ranks in a similar plight all over the country: men who fought so gallantly and endured horrors and deprivations in the worst war mankind has ever known; men whose welfare should be the first consideration of any Government. But what is this Government doing? The pledges given at the last Election to re-house and re-employ returning soldiers are already shown to have been pitifully inadequate. Can we truly claim to be building a land fit for heroes to live in?'

One who inevitably read it was Sir Geoffrey Dillon, the Bellamy family's solicitor, a man of inscrutable temperament and many associations in influential places. The following evening he made one of his rare visits to No. 165 Eaton Place and took his sherry with Richard and Virginia in the morning-room. What he had to propose, in his usual circumlocutory way, provoked Richard into a sharp response.

'Out of the question, Geoffrey. Not even worth discussing.'

'I'm not to take it, am I, that you disapprove of the letter?' Sir Geoffrey's voice had about it its usual oiled-silk smoothness.

'Of course not. I'm simply saying that one letter from a gallant ex-officer doesn't turn him overnight into a peacetime politician.'

He gave Dillon a sharply suspicious glance.

'Look here, Geoffrey – have Central Office sent you here?'

'Good heavens, no. I've no . . . official connection with Central Office. But certain people have let it be known they're interested in James. I'm surprised if no one has spoken to you about it.'

'Well, there have been congratulations, of course, and the subject has been . . . mentioned, here and there. But I dismissed it right away.'

'Wasn't that being a little hasty?' Virginia asked.

'No, my darling, it is not being hasty. I know what's behind this as well as Geoffrey does. The boy is intelligent, he's won an M.C. That carries its own aura. The Conservative Party simply want to use him to enhance their own prestige. But what happens when he gets in? He has no experience of government affairs. He won't know how to make a speech. He'd never survive.'

'He's survived worse.'

'I tell you, he's an amateur. He has no training for the life.'

'Don't you really mean that he's your son, and you're afraid of what people might say about favours?'

'Nonsense, darling. If I really believed he had something to offer, I'd back him to the hilt.'

Dillon intervened, 'I understand your feelings, Richard. But don't you think the Party and the country need new blood?'

Virginia agreed warmly, 'I quite agree with Sir Geoffrey. Anyway, James has lived in an atmosphere of politics in this house all his life. Isn't that sufficient training for the life?'

Before Richard could defend his attitude the door opened and James came in, as briskly as his limp would permit. Sir Geoffrey rose automatically to the master of the house.

'Hello!' James said cheerfully. 'What's this? Not financial trouble, I hope?'

'No, James. I just called in to congratulate you on your letter, and . . .' He hesitated and turned to Richard. 'May I tell him?'

'If you must,' Richard scowled. 'I can't stop you.'

'Tell me what, Sir Geoffrey?'

'Have you ever seriously thought about going into politics?'

James laughed incredulously. 'Me? Good lord, no!' He went to pour himself a drink. Richard ranged his glance from Virginia to Dillon. 'There you are, see?' he said quietly.

Over his shoulder James asked, 'What's all this about, anyway?' His father answered, 'Geoffrey has what amounts to a proposition from Conservative Central Office.'

Dillon was about to protest, but James had turned with his filled glass. 'What? On the strength of one letter? Scribbled in haste? They must be hard up for candidates.'

'They are,' Dillon agreed. 'Of the right sort.'

Virginia said, 'Young men who fought. Who can truly represent the interests of ex-Servicemen and their families.'

'But my letter was supposed to be attacking the Government.'

'The Coalition Government,' Dillon reminded him. 'Not the Conservative Party. The Coalition won't last for ever.'

'I should hope not. Well! I must say, it's an intriguing idea. Would I be tied to the Party line, or could I speak my mind?'

'I think you'd be free to say whatever you liked – assuming you'd support the Party's basic principles.'

'The principles, yes. But not always the way they go about things.'

James sat, as his father rose to pour himself a further drink.

'What do you say, Father? I've been looking for something to do with my idle life.'

Richard paused. 'I'm strongly against the idea, James, as I've made quite clear to Virginia and Geoffrey. When you speak of filling your idle life, I'm delighted you should feel well enough to be ready to do something. Politics is a serious business, not to be entered into light-heartedly . . .'

'Am I giving that impression? Father, I do believe you're jealous.'

Dillon saw his chance. 'Of course, if the life turns out to be not to your taste . . .'

'Or if I fail to get in,' James corrected.

Now Richard turned on Dillon. 'Of course he'll get in. That's not in doubt. The question is, what does he do afterwards? He'll find himself in an entirely false position, handling constituency problems, making speeches. It's a job for professionals.'

James said seriously, 'With all respect, Father, you weren't a professional at the start.'

Richard had to admit to himself the truth of this. His mind flew back swiftly over his own youthful uncertainty and lack of purpose; of the chance way in which he had come to the attention of Benjamin Disraeli, who had instilled into his mind the idea of a political career, and, with the aid of Lord Southwold – and, not least, Lord Southwold's daughter Marjorie, Richard's first love and first wife – had shaped his future for him. He had been so long in politics now that he had forgotten ever having been a novice at it. He considered James unfitted; but how fitted had he himself once been?

James was continuing, without rancour. 'I do take your point, Father. But if I have an opportunity I must be allowed to decide for myself.' He turned to Dillon. 'If I agree, how would I go about it?'

Sir Geoffrey permitted himself a faint smirk. 'There's to be a by-election soon. Old Harry Weatherall, who contested the seat unsuccessfully for years, died last month at seventy-three. It's Barking East.'

'Barking! That's dockland, isn't it?'

'Yes it is,' Richard snapped impatiently. 'A cast-iron Labour seat. Really, Geoffrey, he'd stand no chance there at all. If he really wants to get in, let's for Heaven's sake find him somewhere safe.'

'No, Father,' James said, quite sharply. 'I wouldn't want that.'

Dillon let the objection hang on the air for a moment before putting in, 'Plenty of ex-Servicemen, homeless, unemployed, in Barking, I should imagine. Interesting to see what impression could be made.'

'Very little, I should think,' Richard growled. James turned to his stepmother to ask, 'Virginia, you've been very quiet. What do you think about it all?'

She looked from him to Richard, then back again. 'Well . . . for what my opinion's worth, I think you should do it, if you want to. Richard, I don't want to seem disloyal to you, but quite frankly I find your objections impossible to fathom. There's no great mystique to politics. It's not some exclusive club. If a man, from any walk of life, has an honest and sincere wish to serve his fellow men, then we should encourage him as much as we can.'

'There are other ways,' Richard said flatly, anticipating the usual defeat. James told him earnestly, 'Father, I promise you I'm not going to take this lightly. But I believe I've started something with this demand letter which I have an obligation to see through. Politics is the way you

35

chose, so why shouldn't I? It's in my blood, both sides of the family. I feel fit now – energetic. Perhaps I've just been waiting for the right moment.'

Pausing first to see whether Richard would reply, Sir Geoffrey Dillon asked James, 'May I tell them you're interested? The local association are vetting the applicants this week.'

'You can do more than that. Tell them, if they want me, I'm game.'

Sir Geoffrey positively beamed, like a gratified cat. 'Splendid! Well, I really must go. You know, I think I detect a new influence in this house. Yes – this room's been redecorated, for a start.'

Virginia smiled. 'I hope you approve, Sir Geoffrey.'

He could not suppress a non-committal little sniff. 'We must all move with the times, I suppose.'

'I should hope so,' Virginia said, moving to the door with him.

A few days later, James came in out of the rain, one dark late afternoon, to announce that he had been adopted as prospective Tory Member of Parliament for Barking East. At Virginia's prompting, Richard sent down for champagne.

Two visitors were below stairs when the news of the Major's adoption was received. They were, again, Edward and Daisy, bedraggled with walking through the downpour and distinctly more subdued in manner than when they had last called. Mrs Bridges, as welcoming as ever, placed them before the fire and ordered Ruby to make tea. Mr. Hudson's greeting when he came downstairs and found them was enough to counteract the welcome warmth.

'What are you both doing here?' he asked unsmilingly.

'Just . . . just passin', Mr. Hudson,' Daisy said tensely.

'Yeh,' Edward supported her. 'Thought we'd look in. See how you all was.'

Mr. Hudson could see all too plainly that it was not only damp that had made their clothes so unkempt-looking. Edward's suit was frayed and almost threadbare in places, and Daisy's shoes were not only sodden, but cracked open. She saw his gaze on them.

'Actually, it was Rose we really come to see. Wasn't it, Eddy?'

'Yeh. Dais thinks she left a . . . a pair of winter shoes here, and we thought if Rose's kept them we'd pick 'em up.' He forced a laugh. 'No point in spending on a new pair.'

'No, indeed,' Hudson replied, and told them curtly of the circumstances of Rose's absence. 'But Lily can find the shoes for you,' he concluded.

Daisy said hastily, 'No, no, don't worry, Lily. They're . . . probably lost, after all this time.'

Edward said heavily, 'Well, we'd better be getting back to Camberwell . . .'

'No you won't,' Mrs. Bridges ordered, bustling about. 'They're staying for supper – aren't they, Mr. Hudson?' Giving him no chance to reply, one way or the other, she ordered, 'Lily, lay two places extra.'

Edward and Daisy looked unhappily at one another, but were glad to obey.

'Anything come of that furniture job out Romford way?' Frederick asked Edward a little later, his voice betraying something of his resentment over Edward's earlier boasting about having cut himself free of the bonds of 'service'.

'Oh, that! No, I didn't get that, actually. Fell through, you know.'

'Still selling brushes, then?'

'That's it.'

'Going all right, is it?'

'Up and down. Bad weather doesn't help.'

His embarrassment was obvious, even though he tried to cover it with a feebly humorous anecdote about one of his door-to-door calls. The eternally tactless Ruby had a more hurtful, though innocently meant, question to ask Daisy.

'Whatever happened about your baby, Daisy?'

'Quiet, Ruby,' hissed Mrs. Bridges, who had wondered the same thing as soon as she had seen Daisy's slimmer figure, but had drawn her own conclusions and kept her mouth shut. Daisy said, trying to sound casual, 'Oh, it's all right. You have to know some time. I lost it. Miscarriage. Six months.'

Mrs. Bridges paused to give the thin, damp shoulder a little pat. 'I'm very sorry, Daisy. Truly.'

'Yes,' they heard Mr. Hudson say. 'So am I, Daisy. A great shame.'

'Well, it was disappointing – 'specially for Eddie. But the doctor says I'd be able to have another one. Plenty of time.'

'Course there is,' Mrs. Bridges agreed, but she secretly wiped the corner of each eye as she went to fetch the supper.

The arrival of rabbit pie – 'Just like old times, Mrs. B.!' Edward cried – improved the atmosphere somewhat. Mr. Hudson noted how ravenously he ate.

With genuine curiosity Lily asked Daisy, who was also eating eagerly, 'You got any regrets, leavin' service, Daisy?'

Edward had to answer for his wife, whose mouth was full. 'No regrets, Lily. Just . . . happy memories.'

Daisy managed to mutter, 'Yes. We live on 'em.'

'What do you mean, Daisy?' Mr. Hudson was unable to prevent himself asking.

'Nothing, Mr. Hudson . . .' Edward began, but Daisy threw down her knife and fork and said, near to tears, 'Why keep pretending, Eddie? They aren't fooled.'

Hudson said gently, 'I think we have guessed the truth haven't we, Edward?'

Edward looked at his wife, but she didn't raise her head, only said, 'Tell 'em. For pity's sake.' He looked round the table, then put his own knife and fork on his plate and explained haltingly: 'I think . . . what Dais wants me to say is . . . brush selling didn't work out. I'm out of a job . . . at the moment. But I'll get something else. Can't keep us down for long, can they, Dais . . . ? Oh, Dais . . . don't . . . please!'

38

She was crying openly, fiercely. 'I'm sorry . . . but they're so cruel to people like my Eddie, and I get so angry. Stupid hoity-toity women and butlers shoutin' rude things, slammin' the door in his face. Don't they know what he did for 'em out there? What he went through?'

'Shut up, Dais,' Edward ordered pleadingly. 'They don't want to hear about that.'

'Well, they should hear about it. They're our friends. They're the only friends we got!'

The following pause, broken only by her weeping, was broken by Mr. Hudson, blundering in with, 'We do sympathise, Edward. It's a strange and cruel world. But you did make your own bed, the pair of you . . .'

Edward's restraint went. 'Yes. I remember what you said to us when we was leaving. You wanted us to stop here, rest of our lives, like Rose. Well, me and Dais wanted something better. I reckoned we'd earned it. Only, Dais is right. You don't know what it's like out there in the rotten world, because you never tried it. And until you do, you got no right accusing us . . .'

'Eddie, don't . . . ! Daisy tried, but he went on: 'He hasn't, Dais. He wants to try looking for work, and supporting a wife in a miserable little room with the rain coming in. That's why she lost her baby,' he told them all. 'Because it wasn't possible, the way we was living.' He rounded on Mr. Hudson again, though still speaking to the rest of them. 'He's just a smug, self-satisfied old man, who didn't do nothing in the war except serve bleedin' sherry!''

He threw back his chair and stumbled from the table to where their coats hung. Daisy, with a fearful glance at the ashen-faced Hudson, joined him, and together they went quickly out by the back door, slamming it behind them, leaving only an intense silence over which the hiss and drip of the rain could be heard from the area.

The rain relented next morning, but it was again a dank, drab day to herald James's first appeal to his potential constituents.

The place chosen for him by his agent, Arthur Knowles, an experienced campaigner in his mid-forties, was a street corner close to a dockyard entrance. Tenement buildings overshadowed the site. Occasionally a women came to one or another of the windows to shake out a rug, look down with mild curiosity at the setting up of the flimsy platform and the banners exhorting them to VOTE TORY, or VOTE BELLAMY, or even to MAKE BRITAIN A LAND FIT FOR HEROES, before disappearing again and slamming the windows firmly against the clammy air.

The 'crowd' so far consisted of two dejected-looking women, an old soldier on a crutch, some ragged children, and a dog whose expression displayed, if anything, more interest than any of the humans.

'You sure this is a good spot?' James asked, surveying his audience.

Knowles grinned knowingly and gestured towards the dockyard. 'They'll come through those gates in a minute for their dinner hour. The pensions office is just round the corner, so we should draw the Servicemen. And the women will come out of the buildings.'

James sighed. 'Am I preaching to the employed or the unemployed, then?'

'Preaching?'

'It feels rather like a revivalist meeting.'

Knowles produced a small brandy flash from his coat pocket. 'Here, Major, have a drop of this. Mr. Weatherall always used to loosen his tongue before he spoke.'

James sipped gratefully and felt marginally more assured. He handed back the flask and accepted a tin megaphone.

'I'd start now,' Knowles advised. 'Good luck.'

James nodded and raised the megaphone with his right hand, finding to his consternation that it meant his squinting over to the left to see his notes, and wondering how he would manage to turn the sheets with one hand.

'Good morning!' he cried, putting practised heartiness into it, and startled himself by the noise his amplified voice made and the echo it produced off the grey walls. 'Good morning. I am . . . I am your Conservative Party candidate, James Bellamy. I'm asking for your support at this coming by-election, but first I want to introduce myself to you and explain my reasons for standing here today.'

His audience at this point increased dramatically – virtually doubled itself, in fact – as two men, obviously ex-Servicemen, rounded the corner and paused to listen, and another woman who had chanced to open her window did not immediately withdraw, but stayed leaning on the sill.

Directing his megaphone at the men, James went on.

'Most of my life I have been a professional soldier. Now, it's sometimes said that soldiers should stick to what they know and shouldn't meddle with politics. I believed that once. But these times we're living through – the aftermath of this terrible war in which we've all suffered – they've caused me to change my mind. The gallant working men of this country, with whom I fought in the trenches and whom I gained an undying respect for, I believe they deserved a better deal than they're getting at the moment. Decent housing, proper employment, higher wages . . .'

A drift of men came from the dock gates, but did little more than pause to look James up and down before moving on, their waiting dinners of more interest to them than yet another ration of political hot air. The woman at the open window withdrew her head. The listening ex-Servicemen trudged away. Only the children and the dog remained; but James ploughed on.

'Central Office are rather concerned about him,' Sir Geoffrey Dillon reported to Richard and Virginia one evening later in the week. 'Or rather, the local association, mainly. They've passed on some criticisms.'

'And you've been sent here to pass them on to us,' Richard said. 'Well, come on, Geoffrey, be specific.'

'One example – he's taken rather an unorthodox line on housing. He wants cheap, jerry-built houses by the thousands, it seems, and he doesn't care who pays for them. When it's pointed out that he'd merely be creating the slums of the future he says the future must take care of itself.'

'Can't it?' Virginia demanded.

'No, I take Geoffrey's point,' Richard nodded. 'The Coalition Government's housing policy is the same as the Conservative Party's. By coming out with this stuff he alienates his supporters and puts himself at his opponents' mercy.'

Dillon told her, 'There were even cries of "Communist" at one of his Tory Club meetings. Ironic, I know. But I'm afraid the feeling is growing that he's out of his depth.'

Richard raised his shoulders and let them drop meaningfully. 'It was you who pushed him into the deep end, Geoffrey. You can't blame the boy now.'

'Good heavens, no. I'm merely suggesting he needs a little advice. That's why I've spoken to you, rather than to James.'

'We'll see what we can do,' Richard promised; 'but I rather think I'm the last person he'll listen to.'

Before Sir Geoffrey could speak again James had come briskly into the room. The lawyer muttered something about urgent business, greeted James briefly, and saw himself out. James poured himself a large whisky and sipped thankfully, looking at Richard and Virginia over the rim of his glass.

'What did the old fox want?'

'Just to see how you were getting on,' Virginia answered.

'He could have asked me.'

'You weren't here.'

'So, what did you tell him?'

'Only what you've told us. How did it go today?'

James answered confidently, 'Not badly. Beginning to break through the barriers of apathy. Oh, and I caught sight of my Labour opponent, Harry Shadbolt. No charm at all, as far as I could see. I discovered he didn't fight – lung trouble or something. That's a help.'

Virginia and Richard exchanged glances as he passed them, to sit on the settee. James added, 'We're holding a big open meeting on the day before the poll, in a Seaman's Mission Hall. A final rallying call.'

'Wednesday?' Virginia said. 'May we come?'

Richard said quickly, 'If you felt it would help, I'm prepared to speak . . .'

As if he had anticipated the offer – which he had – James replied promptly, 'Thank you, Father, but I don't want to draw any more attention to my background than the Press are doing already. It doesn't help much, I'm afraid.'

'Then we can easily get someone else . . .'

'I want to do this on my own.'

'My dear boy, no one has ever fought a campaign entirely on his own.'

'Please, Father, I don't want to sound churlish, but I can't think of anyone in the Party who'd be much use to me. Not down there.'

'That's nonsense. There's Austen Chamberlain, Stanley Baldwin . . .'

James got to his feet in a way that left no doubt about his wish to end the discussion. 'Look, I've had a very exhausting day. I'm whacked, and I've got a lot of work to do yet.'

Accepting the dismissal, Richard turned to the door. 'Yes. Well . . . Virginia and I are going to the theatre. Are you coming to change, my dear?'

'Yes, darling. In a moment.'

Richard nodded and went out. James tossed back the last of his drink and went to pour another.

'Can't he realise?' he said. 'They're all the same old men hanging on to pre-war notions. Can't they see the gulf there is now?'

'Yes, of course they can – and they have all their wisdom and experience to bridge it. No, I'm sorry, James, you can't expect me to side with you against Richard all the time. I know what his feelings were to begin with, but since your nomination he's done all he can to support you.'

'Huh! He offers me the kind of advice that would be very useful if I were fighting some safe seat in Gloucestershire.'

43

His stepmother's eyes flashed, and her Scottish accent seemed suddenly more pronounced as she retorted, 'You don't know that, because you haven't listened to him. He's been here every night, with a lifetime's experience behind him, longing for you to discuss your problems. Only, you shut him out, and then have the gall to accuse him of being a meddling old man. Quite apart from the hurt you're causing, I think you're being thoroughly pig-headed.'

James, who had physically recoiled before this tirade, stared silently for a moment before saying, 'I admire your loyalty, Virginia. I understand how things may seem to you. But you don't know everything that's been going on. I have to fight the local Conservative association, my own damn people, day after day.'

'We do know that, James,' she said quietly, and touched his arm in a peacemaking gesture. 'We hear things, and it seems to me you need friends. Well, your father is the best friend you've got. So just think about it, will you?'

Without waiting for an answer she went off to go upstairs and change.

On the Tuesday evening Edward and Daisy paid a further visit to the house. Their manner was distinctly subdued and embarrassed.

The day following the earlier contretemps, Frederick had called at their lodgings, bringing a note from Mrs. Bridges and pair of worn but sound winter shoes. Defiant to Edward's protests that they weren't reduced to accepting charity, Daisy had insisted on trying on the shoes. They fitted perfectly. Near to hysteria, Edward had threatened to leave her if she wouldn't give them back. She had refused, and her husband had had to relieve his feelings by almost throwing Frederick out through the door, which he had then slammed and leant against, weeping.

It had been a further note from Mrs. Bridges that had brought them round now, for tea. Her sleep had been troubled at the thought of their plight and on receipt of a polite note of thanks from Daisy for the shoes she had impulsively invited them, though not without asking the approval of Mr. Hudson, who had answered stiffly that she was, of course, free to invite any guests of her own she might choose. He would have preferred not to have been present himself, but his duties prevented his going out. He and Edward greeted one another formally and warily, and when Edward tried to put together an apology for his behaviour the butler silenced him with the opinion that the subject was best left alone. At least, Daisy was now comfortably dry-shod.

They sat uneasily at the table in the servants' hall, waiting for tea, Mr. Hudson self-consciously and unnecessarily polishing his spectacles, Edward and Daisy exchanging halting conversation with Mrs. Bridges and Lily, while Ruby made the tea in the kitchen. Frederick came in, in his green uniform. Addressing Mr. Hudson, he announced, 'Her ladyship would like to see Edward and Daisy before they go.'

'Us!' Edward exclaimed. 'What for?'

Hudson looked up. 'I suggest you go up now, before tea, rather than keep her ladyship waiting.'

Apprehensively, they obeyed, and some moments later were standing side by side, like a pair of errant children, as Virginia came across the morning-room towards them.

'It must be over a year since you left here, isn't it?' she said, in a tone calculated to allay whatever fears they might be feeling.

Daisy answered, 'Fourteen months, my lady.'

'So long? Where are you living now?'

'Small room in Camberwell, m'lady,' Edward said.

'Well it occurred to me . . . the flat above the garage is empty. It hasn't been occupied since Mr. and Mrs. Watkins left, before the war. You remember them?'

'I do, m'lady,' Edward said, suddenly dry-mouthed. 'Daisy wasn't here then.'

'I see. Well, it seems ideal for a married couple, and such a waste. Also, we need a chauffeur. Can you drive, Edward?'

He could scarcely manage to reply, 'Yes, m'lady. I learnt in the war.'

'Good.' She turned to the wide-eyed Daisy. 'We also need another housemaid, especially at the moment with Rose away. And when she comes back she'll be my personal maid, so that wouldn't affect you.' Quite matter-of-factly she added, 'Lily would be under you.'

Permitted a natural instinct, Edward and Daisy would have fallen into one another's arms; but Daisy just said, 'Thank you ever so much, my lady.'

As though uninterrupted, Virginia went on, 'Frederick will continue as footman and will also valet his lordship. But the Major needs a valet, so it would be helpful if you could combine your duties, Edward.'

As he mumbled his thanks she was already moving to ring the bell. Daisy could hold back tears no longer. 'We're so grateful, m'lady. We . . . we'll work ever so hard. Really . . .'

They heard the door open behind them. 'Hudson,' Lady Bellamy was saying, 'Edward and Daisy are willing to come back into service. It was a good idea of yours, thank you.'

'Thank *you*, my lady,' the astonished young couple heard the butler reply; but as they turned to go they could read nothing in his features nor in the eyes which did not seem to notice them as they passed.

'Yes, Hudson told me,' James said to his father next day, when Richard mentioned, for want of a conversational opening, that Edward and Daisy would be rejoining the staff. 'I'm very pleased.'

James was dressed in a quiet, perfectly-cut city suit, with a blue and white rosette in one lapel and an un-ostentatious buttonhole in the other. He had been making the last revisions to his notes for the open meeting. His father, all uncertainty, turned to leave the room again, but James said, almost blurting it out, 'Father, I'm sorry if I've seemed . . . high-handed, these past weeks. It wasn't really meant or . . . directed against you personally. I somehow, quite wrongly, lumped you with certain Party attitudes, and . . .'

'You don't need to apologise, James.'

'I had to prove myself, you see.'

'I understand.'

'Do you . . . would you come to the meeting today?'

Richard hesitated. 'Virginia and I had planned to go to the Leicester Galleries to see the Epstein sculptures.'

'I'd like you to come,' James said, quietly, looking down at his notes.

'Both of us?'

'Both of you.'

Richard smiled at last. 'It'll be a pleasure.'

'I wouldn't count on it. I'm having trouble with this damned speech. Would you . . . look at it . . . please?'

Still smiling, Richard took it without a word and sank into the settee, fishing with his free hand for his spectacles and already frowning with the effort to read before he had got them on.

'. . . During the two weeks I've been among you . . .'

Whistles and boos. '*Two weeks!*'

'. . . I've been impressed by many things. By the industry and dedication of the dock workers . . .'

'*Hurray!*'

'. . . striving to get this country back on to its feet . . .'

'Wot – wiv the bleedin' Tories!'

'. . . and the fortitude . . .'

'The Tories are the enemies of the working classes!' That damned woman again, tall and sharp-faced, her hair scraped back, her accent anything but working-class. James waited patiently for the cheers and boos which her every intervention – and they were constant – provoked in this almost packed hall. He went on. 'Yes, the fortitude of those of you who are unemployed – many of you ex-Servicemen – in what must be the most disheartening circumstances . . .'

An eruption of catcalls and suggestions greeted this. Seated at the back of the hall, unobtrusively dressed, Richard and Virginia held hands tightly. Edward, who had chauffered them all there, stood nearby, feeling the sweat running into the collar of the smart uniform which, he was all too conscious, had attracted suspicious looks from several of the heavily-built dockers around him.

James was forging on gallantly, and not without support. But it was apparent that the general mood of the meeting was against him and the cause for which he stood, not least because of the well-rehearsed interventions of the woman heckler. Unbeknown to him, she had been one of the earliest to arrive at the Seaman's Mission, with the purpose of securing the position which she knew from long practice would give her more command of the meeting than any platform speaker.

When James produced a copy of his pamphlet, which hopeful supporters had proffered at the hall door and earned more coarse jibes than thanks as a result, the conduct of the meeting seemed to become reversed, with the woman making the speech and James endeavouring to intervene.

'Upper class propaganda!' she yelled.

'In this pamphlet, I repeat, I have tried to lay down . . .'

'Down with the class system! The workers are the wage slaves of their employers. We want common ownership. Abolish the social classes!'

'Madam . . .' James shouted over the mixture of cheers and boos, '. . . the spirit of co-operation and fellowship between all classes which was built up in the war has to be maintained if we . . .'

This time the professional agitator's work was done for her by a spontaneous mixture of male and female cries from all parts of the hall.

'We don't want to hear about the war!'

'Enough of the bloody war!'

'Blame the war for everything!'

One voice amongst them all brought a deep flush to

James's face: 'Where'd you get your bleedin' medal? Sittin' in some chateau behind the lines?' Richard's grip tightened on Virginia as he felt her move to get up. James was telling the heckler, clearly furious but not without control on his temper: 'I risked my life for you to say that! You can't ignore the war as if it never happened . . .'

'Don't you accuse us!' a woman cried shrilly, to sympathetic cries. 'I 'ad two sons and a 'usband die for this rotten country.'

'Yer!' a gigantic man standing almost next to Edward bellowed. 'You're not one of us.'

Stung, James called back, 'No man under my command in the trenches ever said that!'

This was adjudged highly hilarious, with questions to him as to whether he thought he was 'Douglas-bloody Haig' or which other war leader. In one part of the hall a slight scuffle broke out but was quickly quelled by one of the few policemen present. James tried to salvage the situation.

'To move on to one of the most important issues – housing . . .'

It was like lighting the fuse of a firework, or pulling the pin of a grenade.

'You gotter nice 'ouse, 'ave yer?'

''ow many bleedin' rooms?'

''ow many bloody servants?'

'I want more houses for the *people*,' James insisted, before being howled down again.

'Please, ladies and gentlemen,' cried Arthur Knowles, whose expression in the last moments had been growing increasingly dismayed. 'Please let your candidate speak.'

The militant young woman, who had been studiedly conserving her energies while others were unwittingly serving her cause, now returned in full voice.

'He's got nothing to say. There's only one way to save this country, and that is by revolution!' Undeterred by the rising tide of booing this alien sentiment provoked, she continued, 'Follow the lead of Russia! Smash the greedy

49

Capitalists! Send them back to the barbaric ages where they belong!'

Amidst the uproar another female voice was heard now. Seated beside its owner, Richard Bellamy felt himself almost numbed to realise that it was Virginia's. She was on her feet, waving one arm, commanding, through sheer surprise and urgency, the attention of the people who had turned astonished faces in wonder at these cultivated Scots tones.

'You don't want Communism,' she was yelling at them. 'You've had enough of fighting. And that's what a Bolshevik revolution would mean. Now's the time for unity, for working together. Not disruption, not strikes. Ignore the hotheads, the enemies of this country. Vote for peace and prosperity. *Vote for Bellamy!*'

Richard, almost succumbing to the temptation to bury his face in his hands, couldn't help recalling a political clamour about his own ears, long ago, touched off by a woman who had loved him. But this was very different. After a second or two of hesitation, and a few cries of support for Virginia and for the staring candidate on the platform, the rehearsed rioting began; the specially-gathered tomatoes from the gutters of the street market-places were produced and hurled platform-wards; the crowds began to surge, and the police moved forward.

Edward, heavily jostled, interpreted Richard's signal and slipped out to where the car was waiting. Richard flung an arm round his wife and edged her towards the door. What seemed to be a menacing wall of gigantic dockers almost surrounded them; but their emotions were directed at more distant objectives, and, with the aid of a bearded police constable who seemed possessed of the strength of ten, the couple escaped into the night, to reach the car at the same moment as an infuriated James and his shaken agent. They could hear the racket in the hall until they had driven the length of the street in which it stood.

At his end of the long servants' table Mr. Hudson cleared

his throat for silence. A newspaper, just put into his hand by Frederick, was folded to an item prominent on the front page. Frederick resumed his seat beside Lily. Mrs. Bridges, Edward, Daisy and Ruby watched, awed, as Mr. Hudson began to declaim in the portentous tones of any Returning Officer, the result of the by-election:

'Bellamy, Conservative, seven thousand three hundred and sixty-nine votes.' (Gasps of approval.) 'Macneill, Socialist Labour Party, one thousand and forty-three votes' (a quickly-silenced cry of 'He's won!' from Lily), 'Shadbolt, Labour – eighteen thousand nine hundred and twenty-eight votes.' Mr. Hudson nearly added, 'And I declare the said . . .', but quickly changed it to, 'Mr. Shadbolt is duly elected to Parliament.'

Before lunch, Richard, Virginia and Sir Geoffrey Dillon drank sherry and tried in vain to persuade James that he had fought courageously and with dignity, had not disappointed his predecessor's staunch supporters, and – Richard's sentiments – gained invaluable experience and proved to him and to others that the necessary qualities were there for some other occasion. James merely shook his head, his cloak of despondency donned once more, almost welcomingly.

'I didn't do well at all. I failed. But it's not the result that upsets me. It's what I saw with my own eyes – what I heard. I believed there was one spark of hope – just one – that came from the hideous waste of that war. That was the courage, the fellowship, the sheer bloody good sense that officers like me saw for the first time in the working man. I believed if we could just hold that common ground, keep trusting each other, we could build something in peacetime. But what happens? We become two nations again. Back to the old entrenched positions.'

He got up from the chair in which he had been slumped and went to stand facing his father.

'What did we have to offer them, Father – *our* Party? What a pathetic lot we are, skulking behind Lloyd George's Coalition, complacently biding our time . . . Well, if ever that time comes, I can tell you there won't be a country left worth governing. All decency, all traditional values gone – vanished without trace.'

He turned to Dillon.

'You can tell Central Office, Sir Geoffrey, I won't be standing again. And now if you'll excuse me, Father, Virginia, I really don't think I can face lunch. If anyone wants me I'll be at the Guards' Club.'

Before anyone could say anything he was across the room and at the door, reaching it just as Hudson entered.

'I shan't be lunching in today, Hudson,' James said. 'I'm going to my club.'

'Very good, sir. May I, er, on behalf of the staff, sir, offer our sincere congratulations on your reducing the Labour majority . . .'

James halted, turned, and stared.

'Did I ?'

'Yes indeed, sir. By six hundred or so votes from the last General Election. It was a notable achievement, sir.'

For the first time that day, James smiled.

'Thank you, Hudson.'

Without a look at the others he strode out. Hudson turned towards Virginia.

'Luncheon is served, m'lady.'

CHAPTER THREE

EDWARD and Daisy had been lucky; many more were not. The search for work, for decent homes, for bare subsistence, even, remained the only full-time occupation of tens of thousands of disenchanted men and women who had played their part in winning the 'war to end all wars'.

The hardship was by no means confined to those on humbler social levels. In some ways, these were less hard hit than their former 'betters'; having never had much in life, they had less to feel deprived of and found it easier to make the best of meagre allowances and assistance. Worst afflicted of all, perhaps, were the middle-class and self-made men who had worn officers' uniform. Their brief authority and privilege at an end, they had to try to merge into the surroundings from which they had originally come, but for many it was no easy thing to do. Either they could not swallow their acquired dignity and return to humdrum tasks, often under the orders of men who had held common rank, or no rank at all; or they found their jobs usurped by others, or simply vanished; or their own natures, made restless by their years out of context, would not let them settled down, but kept them moving from one thing to another, always searching for they knew not what, and never finding it.

One of the latter was a friend of Georgina's, Robin Eliot, a well-built, fair-haired youth a year or two younger than she, of unfailingly good-humoured disposition. To anyone who passed him in the street, or saw him roar by on his indispensable motor-bike, he gave the impression of being one of the war's luckier survivors. His daytime suits were immaculately pressed and groomed, and almost every night saw him in full evening dress, as often as not dancing with Georgina and a varying party of her friends at the Berkeley or some other fashionable rendezvous. His father was known to have an estate in Wiltshire, and Robin himself had all the appearances of a carefree ex-captain with a full wallet and a rewarding future that merely awaited his making the effort to catch up with it.

The truth was very different. Although it was by now the autumn of 1921 and he had got his discharge almost a year before, he had been able to find no work anything like commensurate with his standing as a minor gentleman. He was qualified for nothing; he possessed neither outstanding intelligence nor the quick-wittedness which can be even more valuable, when it comes to making opportunities against the odds; and the father who would gladly have helped him was himself on the verge of bankruptcy and about to sell his estate for less than it needed to pay all his debts.

What Robin would not do, though, was to give up his social life. Increasingly, it seemed to him to be the one thing left to cling on to before circumstances washed him away; and increasingly, too, he saw Georgina as his personal last refuge. While he could still dance at the Berkeley – where, given the right clothes and company, one could do so for very little actual expenditure – he was all right. He knew that once he had to start making excuses for not joining in, he would never be able to face them or her again.

He swallowed his pride and took what jobs he could get, and made no effort to conceal them from his fashionable friends, playing instead the role of a jokey adventurer who didn't care what he did during the day because he only lived for the evenings. They laughed hugely with him when he told them he was selling brushes – the very trade at which Edward had failed utterly – and shared his merriment when, within a few weeks, he recounted, with a wealth of anecdote, the downward course of his own failure at it, mentioning no word of the many humiliations he had experienced. They were positively convulsed by his story, a week or two later, of an even more diastrous door-to-door round, trying to sell haircurlers on behalf of a wartime profiteer who had become a British national only just before the war.

Still the evenings at the Berkeley continued; and several times Robin asked Georgina to marry him. She took it as just another facet of his joking and refused to answer anything but flippantly. To her surprise, at a fancy dress party, he got her alone and asked her again, obviously earnestly this time. When she refused, he let his guise slip for the first and only time, and almost pleaded that everyone needed someone to hang on to.

'I don't want to have anyone to hang on to,' Georgina said unsympathetically. 'I'm awfully fond of you, Robin, but I don't want to spend the rest of my life with you and nobody else.'

She didn't notice how pale he was as he said, deliberately, 'I love you Georgina. I can't live without you.'

'Oh, it's too sick-making to hear boring and stupid things like that!' she exclaimed, and flounced away.

Ten minutes later he shot himself dead in a cupboard.

A note in his hand was addressed to her as 'Dearest Georgina'. Fortunately for her, the person who reached him first concealed and then destroyed it, and her name was not mentioned in the newspapers. She made a determined attempt to act as if the incident had not affected her at all; but James, who had often talked with Robin when he had come to collect Georgina at Eaton Place, saw through her pretence and persuaded her to take up a long-standing invitation to visit his sister Elizabeth and her American husband in that country.

James's personal brand of restlessness was of longer standing. It was part – a major part – of his very personality. It had to a large extent blighted his life, and in varying degrees the lives of almost everyone with whom he had any sort of intimate association. It had brought his father and his late mother much sadness, and his late wife heartbreak. But he remained his own principal victim, and the wartime return to soldiering, which had seemed to come as a blessed release from the boredom of commercial life, had only brought him new bitterness, not to mention physical and mental scars. The unsuccessful flirtation with politics had inevitably added to his disillusionment.

In a way, it was a pity that he was well enough placed financially not to have to take on some humble occupation, which would at least have kept him busy and perhaps done his soul some much-needed good. He spent most of his time prowling restlessly about the house, or listening to his gramophone, or, more rarely, reading the newspapers at his club. He had no long-term ambition, nor even any short-term object: a dangerous state for a man of his temperament.

Richard, entering the morning-room one evening, resplendent in white tie and tails and wearing the orders of a Privy Councillor and the Grand Cross of the Order of St. Michael & St. George, was surprised and at once pleased to see the cheerful expression on his son's face, and the brisk way in which he moved unbidden to pour him a whisky.

'Hello, Father! Where are you off to, all got up like that?'

'A banquet at the Guildhall,' Richard said, accepting the glass. 'If Virginia doesn't make us late, that is.' He glanced at his watch, frowned, and then said, 'Well, what have you been up to today? Looking for a job?'

'No. As I told you, I'm pursuing various lines. I'll tell you when there's any news.'

Richard frowned again. 'I just hope you're not squandering the money Great Aunt Kate left you.'

At most times James would have seized upon this mild caution as an excuse for a petulant outburst. Now, he merely smiled and answered, 'As a matter of fact, I've just spent – *not* squandered – some of that money on something you may regard as an extravagance, but I see as an investment.'

Richard looked at him almost suspiciously. James went on.

'You know I've been having flying lessons at Brooklands.'

'Of course. And got your "A" Certificate.'

'Well, I'm really rather keen on this whole aviation business and its commercial future and . . .'

Richard glanced at the door, wishing Virginia would hurry.

'What are you trying to tell me?'

Sounding like a guilty schoolboy who has spent the change from his shopping errand on sweets, James said, 'I've bought an aeroplane.'

'You've *what*?'

It was easier, now that it was out. 'It's an old two-seater reconnaissance machine, from the Aircraft Disposal Company. An Avro 504. A bit primitive, of course, but absolutely airworthy, and only cost me £275. I took her up today for the first time.'

Richard suppressed a sigh. 'Did you? Well, I suppose you know what you're doing.'

'Of course I do, Father. She handles beautifully – like a thoroughbred hunter with a soft mouth . . .'

Virginia's arrival at that moment cut short the conversation; but the simile between the aircraft and a horse was repeated next morning after breakfast when James came briskly into the morning-room, handsome in jodhpurs, hacking jacket and polo neck jersey, and found his father and stepmother there with the newspapers. Richard had mentioned the aeroplane to Virginia on their way to the Guildhall, and now she questioned James about it, with, he noted, an interest and enthusiasm his father had not displayed.

'Funny thing about riding and flying,' James remarked, having told her all. 'They're really quite alike. My instructor says if you're a good horseman – good hands and a sense of balance – you should make a good pilot.'

'And you're a good horseman,' Virginia said, 'so you must be a good pilot.'

'Well, I don't want to boast, but I *am* pretty good. Got through the course without a mishap and passed my navigation test first time. D'you know, two chaps landed in the sewage farm last week. It's a regular hazard down there – that and the motor-racing track.'

Virginia laughed. 'How fast does your aeroplane go?'

'Oh, 80–90 miles an hour.'

Richard, behind his *Times*, heard James stop suddenly, then say, 'Virginia, I've had a capital idea. It's such a glorious autumn day. Why don't you come down with me and see the old crate? I'll take you up in her, if you like.'

Without hesitation she replied, 'Oh, yes please! I've always wanted to fly.'

They both turned with surprise at the sharpness with which Richard said, 'I don't wish to dampen your enthusiasm, James, but Virginia knows quite well that I'm opening an important debate on Foreign Affairs in the Lords this afternoon.' His annoyed gaze moved to Virginia. 'We arranged last night, you'll recall, that you'd sit with Lady Morling in the Strangers' Gallery and we'd all have tea after the debate.'

Virginia did recall. 'Yes, we did. How depressing.'

James put in, 'Oh, come on, you don't have to, do you? Send word you've got a cold, or something, and come with me.'

His stepmother's answer was a glance at his father, now standing grim-faced.

'Father,' James urged, 'I'm sure Lady Morling won't die of a broken heart if Virginia isn't in the Lords today. It's not always perfect flying weather like this, and she can hear you make a speech any time.'

For one brief instant Richard wondered whether he wasn't being selfish in insisting on his wife's duty to himself. It *was* a beautiful day, and he hated to feel himself the cause of the change of expression on her face from happy excitement to glum acceptance. But his real reason for objecting asserted itself at once: he knew his James and the seeming inevitability with which every point at which he touched life was left bruised. That the boy – the man, nearing middle age, Good Heavens! – was a competent pilot, he didn't doubt, and he expected the machine was sound enough. It was simply that, shameful though it was to admit it, he would trust his wife's safety into many people's hands, but not in those of his own son.

He would never permit himself to put such a hurtful thought into words, however. Instead, he said coldly, 'Virginia is perfectly entitled to choose how she wishes to spend her afternoon. Excuses can be made to the Morlings, if necessary. I merely suggest that it might be more fitting for her to be seen in the Gallery of the House of Lords, when her husband is opening a debate for the Government, than to be seen going up in an aeroplane with her stepson.'

'That's unfair!' Virginia protested, annoyed by the way the pronouncement had sounded, as though she were not even in the room to be consulted.

'What is?'

'To put it all on to me. You know it isn't my decision at all.'

'Do you want me to forbid you to go flying with James – like some stern Victorian husband?'

'I'd almost rather you did. Of course I'd sooner go up in James's machine than sit in the Lords all afternoon. It would be something new. Something to do with the future, not the past.'

A painful silence descended like a fog blanket and hung between them all, until Richard said, 'If you're coming with me to the House, Virginia, we must lunch at one sharp and leave by two-fifteen. I shall be in my study, if you want me.'

He went out, closing the door behind him. Wide-eyed at the schoolmasterly admonition, Virginia turned slowly to James, who said quietly, 'And if you want to come for a joy-ride in my aeroplane, we could leave here at twelve, lunch at Brooklands, and be up in the clear blue sky by two-fifteen. It's for you to say, Virginia. It's your life – not Father's.'

She wandered away to the window, to gaze up at the tempting shimmering blue.

It had not been one of the easiest afternoons below stairs, on account of one new arrival in the household and one relative newcomer.

The latter was Frederick. Startled no less than the female servants by an almighty crash which seemed to come from the butler's pantry, he had rushed to see what was the matter and found Mr. Hudson staring at the dropped tray and scatter of dining-room cutlery at his feet.

'You all right, Mr. Hudson?' Fred asked, genuinely alarmed.

'I . . . the tray fell, that is all.'

'I'll see to it,' Frederick offered, squatting to start picking things up, just as Ruby's vacant face peered round the door.

'What's happened?' she asked.

Hudson twitched angrily. 'Nothing has happened. The tray is too wide for the door, that is all. Go back to the kitchen, girl.'

She went, her parting stare irritating him further.

'You should've let me carry it,' Fred said, well-meaningly. 'It's heavy.'

'Frederick, I have been carrying the butler's tray in and out of this pantry since before you were born.'

'Then it's time you stopped, Mr. Hudson. Let a younger man do the heavy work. You've only to call me when there's something you can't manage . . .'

Hudson erupted. 'Now, you listen to me, Frederick! If you're going to continue as footman here you'll kindly carry out my orders to you and refrain from making suggestions of that nature. In a residence of this size the butler is responsible at all times for the smooth running of the household . . .'

'I was only trying to help, Mr. Hudson. Rose said you wasn't getting any younger, and I was to help you as much as possible.'

'Rose had no business to say that!' Hudson retorted, and Fred retreated, crushed. But he had spoilt Hudson's day.

The other ruffler of domestic tranquillity was Miss Treadwell, the newly-appointed governess to Virginia's

60

children. She had not been encountered in advance by anyone at No. 165, so there had been no chance for report and assessment. Virginia had met her when she had been staying at Harborough Castle, where Miss Treadwell was then in charge of the Honourable Charles Tatham. That young man had now gone away to school, and Virginia had invited the governess to come to London and take charge of Alice and William, over-riding their protests that they were happy enough with things as they were.

Miss Treadwell had not been in the house long before she had made it quite clear what status she proposed to assume. She was in her mid-thirties and not unpleasant to look at, though a prim severity in her face matched her manner. She had been engaged to an officer who had been killed in the war, and since then had worked in aristocratic surroundings. Neither of these was conducive to rapport with ordinary servants. She announced that she would be taking her meals in her room upstairs, or with the children in the dining-room.

'Who's she think she is?' demanded Edward, who had brought her from the station in the car. 'Insisted on sitting behind, 'stead of up front with me.'

'And what's she have to have a tray for?' Ruby asked, laying tea things on it. 'Why can't she eat down here? We could lay a corner of the table.'

'That is out of the question,' Mr. Hudson told her. 'As governess, Miss Treadwell is entitled to her meals in her room, except when she eats with the family.'

'Well, don't expect me to take them up,' Rose snapped, bustling about other duties. 'Daisy can see to all that.'

'I'm not carrying trays up to no governess!' Daisy retorted. 'It's Frederick's place.'

'Don't think I'm the nursery footman!' Fred cautioned them, and received another of Mr. Hudson's reproofs for his pains.

'Now, that's quite enough for one day, Frederick. And all of you, listen to me. I shall assign your duties in consultation with her ladyship and you will carry them out. This is not

61

the kind of household in which we indulge in petty arguments about who is to carry a tray.'

Fred turned away with a wry smile as he recalled the passage of arms about another tray. As he did so he chanced to look out of the window.

'Here!' he exclaimed. 'What's that? Fog?'

'Never!' said Mrs. Bridges, hurrying to peer out into the area. 'It's as bright as . . . Why, I never! You're right, Fred. Must have come down sudden.'

'Cor!' said Edward. 'Can't hardly see the railings.'

Mrs. Bridges turned away with an exasperated click of her teeth.

'Now what's it going to be about dinner? What with his lordship at the House of Lords, and her ladyship and the Major motoring in the country . . .'

'Her ladyship told Miss Treadwell she'd be back by five,' Rose said. 'Because of the children.'

Mr. Hudson looked at his watch. 'Well, it's gone that now. It depends how widespread the fog may be. Best allow for some delay, Mrs. Bridges. If his lordship returns first I will take his instructions.'

Richard did return first. It was after seven, and he told Hudson that his taxi cab had positively crawled the short distance from Westminster. He showed surprise and then annoyance when he was told that no telephone call had been received from the Major and somewhat brusquely told Hudson to find out the number of Brooklands Flying Club and ask for the secretary there.

When Hudson had made the connection and put it through to the morning-room extension he could not restrain himself from listening in. None of the staff had been told the purpose of the motoring expedition and Hudson's expression changed from surprise to incredulity and finally to grave concern as he heard the secretary report to Lord Bellamy that his son had taken off that afternoon in perfectly clear weather, with his stepmother as his passenger, and had not been heard of since.

'Heading for *where*? This line's terrible.'

'South West. Wiltshire. Major Bellamy said he intended showing his stepmother his ancestral home.'

'Southwold! All that way!' Would he have enough petrol?'

'Oh, yes. When we hadn't heard anything by six we telephoned to Southwold. A servant answered and said that a plane flew over at about half-past four. That'd be about right.'

'It didn't land?'

'No. Just circled once or twice, then disappeared into cloud.'

'Is this fog down that way, too?'

'I'm afraid so, Lord Bellamy. Naturally, we've put in calls to all the likely aerodromes, civil and military. I'm afraid there's been no news yet.'

'But surely they must be down somewhere by now.'

'Possibly in a field – anywhere. Major Bellamy's been taught how to pick a safe spot for an emergency landing. He wouldn't stay up after dark, for sure.'

'Well . . . thank you, then. You'll telephone me here the very moment you have any news?'

'Of course, Lord Bellamy. I shouldn't worry, if I were you. Your son has all the resource it needs, judging by the way he swam through his training.'

Hudson waited for the click of the morning-room receiver going down before he replaced the earpiece of the wall telephone below stairs. Then, as was his custom, he made a point of immediately visiting the morning-room on some errand and was rewarded by hearing an account of the conversation from Lord Bellamy himself, thus enabling him to report it to the other servants without having to admit to having eavesdropped.

Lily, whom only that morning Rose had taken it into her head to caution about the Major's old propensity for making advances towards female servants, burst into tears as soon as she heard the news. James had never, in fact, given her so much as an appraising look, but Rose's warning had thrilled her and left her speculating how she really would respond if he ever did make approaches to her. She had started to feel almost proprietorial towards him, as the only female in the house likely to attract his interest if he should start feeling 'that way' inclined; and now it seemed as if he had been taken away from her personally.

'Supposing they're crashed and dead!' she wept.

Hudson, harbouring the same fear, tried to reassure himself as well as comfort her.

'It is all in the hands of the Good Lord, Lily. You must not give way to ungrounded fears. Try to have faith and patience.'

'I am, Mr. Hudson. It's just that I couldn't bear to think of the Major . . . and her ladyship . . . I mean, they're both good, kind souls . . .'

'That is indeed so, Lily. On the other hand, we must all spare a thought for his lordship in his anxiety, while we keep in mind the old saying that no news is good news. Now, dry your eyes, girl, and run along with you.'

Upstairs, Richard paced the morning-room, his feelings a bitter mixture of anxiety that some accident had occurred, irritation that, if none had, neither James nor Virginia had seen fit to telephone to reassure him, and the resentment which had been growing in him ever since he had learned finally that Virginia had decided to break her promise to attend the debate and go chasing off with James.

Fortunately for him, a chance caller was the old family friend Lady Prudence Fairfax, cynical looker-on at so many Society dramas and scandals in her time. She was just the sounding-board he needed for the outpouring of the full range of his feelings.

'That bloody fool of a boy! Irresponsible ass. I blame Virginia, too. She ought to have known better.'

'Richard, dear, you must keep calm,' crooned Lady Prue, giving unspoken thanks that she had chanced to become embroiled in something which might be the talk of everyone's table for the next few days at least.

Her soothing only provoked him into deeper unreason.

'They both know perfectly well we dine at eight o'clock

64

in this house. It's five to eight now. I detest unpunctuality
... keeping the servants hanging about.'

Lady Prue had known him for too many years to rebuke
him. Instead, she calmly suggested that they sit down to
dinner together, and afterwards insisted upon staying with
him as long as might be necessary, even if it meant sleeping
on the settee. When a late hour had been reached with still
no word, Richard tried to make her go home or at least
take one of the bedrooms, but she told him to send the
servants to bed and go up and try to sleep himself. The
telephone should be left connected through to the morning-
room and she would take any call there might come.

Gratefully obedient, for the events of the day on top of the
strain of the debate had produced a fatigue that no amount
of worry could dispel, Richard left her there by the fire,
alone with her thoughts of what might have been, if only
he had needed her after Marjorie's death nearly ten years
ago...

The sound of horse's hooves and the cheery cry of
'Milko!' woke Rose. She raised her eyes blearily, surprised
to find that she had spent the night at the table in the
servants' hall, her head resting on her arms. She shivered
and got up stiffly, noticing simultaneously that it was just
seven o'clock and that Mr. Hudson was asleep in his chair,
his glasses still on his nose and his open book on his knees.

She tiptoed up the stairs, on her way to her first duty,
which was to wake the children. In the hall she met his
lordship coming down, looking rumpled and unshaven.

'Is ... was there any news, my lord?' she asked. He shook
his head.

'Evidently not. Rose, I'm glad to have caught you. You
haven't woken the children yet?'

'No, my lord.'

'Good. Tell Miss Treadwell first that they're not to be
told anything yet. I don't want them upset.'

'Yes, m'lord.'

As Rose went away upstairs the telephone in the morning-room began to ring. Richard hastened in, aware of Prue stirring on the settee. She watched him as he took the call, eagerly at first and then with growing disappointment. His face was set as he put down the instrument at last and turned to her.

'Brooklands. They've had a message from the Coastguard people at Padstow on the North Cornish coast. The lighthouse on Trevose Head reported seeing a small biplane flying low over the sea at about seven o'clock yesterday evening. They couldn't see it clearly for the fog and low cloud, so they weren't sure which direction it was going in. That's all.'

'It can't have been James,' Prue said, sitting up and straightening her hair.

'He could have been off his course.'

'Well, I still think it was some other aeroplane.'

Hudson, who had been awakened by the ringing bell, appeared in the doorway, his face full of frank curiosity.

'Hudson, you'd better tell them downstairs that there's still no news,' Richard said heavily. 'I'd like you all to carry on with your duties as best you can. I shall go up to my dressing-room and shave. Perhaps you'd tell Rose to go up and open the curtains in her ladyship's room. Lady Prudence will need to tidy up in there.'

'Very good, m'lord.'

'We'll breakfast in the dining-room at nine o'clock.'

Breakfast-time came and went with still no news. Twice the telephone rang, and twice it proved to be some call unconnected with the crisis. The third time it started to shrill, Hudson wearily asked Frederick to go and answer it. He had earlier squashed another well-meant effort of the footman's to do one of his tasks for him – Hudson was feeling as tired and drawn as he looked – but now he no longer cared about putting his dignity second. He listened dully as Frederick, unused to telephoning, struggled to hear and shouted back seemingly unnecessarily.

'Pardon? I can't hear you very well. No, the footman speaking. A what? A trunk call? Where from . . .?'

His tiredness forgotten, Hudson sprang to take the receiver, almost wresting it from Frederick's hand and pushing him aside.

'This is Lord Bellamy's butler speaking . . .'

The call was swiftly transferred to the morning-room. From the heightened pitch of Richard's voice and the rapidity of his speech, Prudence could tell that the news was good, though his expression remained grim.

'What time into Paddington? One-seventeen. I understand. Yes, yes, I'll have the train met. I'm most grateful for your help and for letting me know. Goodbye.'

He put down the receiver and turned to Prue, his expression still unchanged.

'They're safe.'

'Thank God. Where?'

'In a train, on their way back from North Cornwall. Newquay, of all places. That was the police. Apparently James lost his bearings in the fog over the West Country. They flew North West from Southwold instead of due East and didn't break through the cloud base until Padstow. The plane ran short of fuel and he had to land it on a deserted beach. They spent the night in it, and this morning James walked four miles to a farm, where there was no telephone. Someone took him into Newquay by pony trap.'

Prudence sighed. 'I'm so very glad it's turned out all right, Richard. I thought it would, but one worries, all the same.'

'Prudence, my dear, you've been a wonderful help. Must you go, though?'

'You've got them back, so I'll retire from the scene. You know you can call on me at any time.'

She kissed him on the cheek and turned towards the door.

'Anyway, I've got my Unmarried Mothers' Committee, so I couldn't have stayed, anyway. Just give them my love.'

'I will.'

'But tell James that if he insists on flying his wretched machine he should fly it round and round the aerodrome by himself. Some of us are getting too old for scares like that.'

She let herself out. A few moments later Hudson entered, to be told the good news by a surprisingly grim-faced Lord Bellamy.

'How dare you do this to me? Damn you! Both of you!'

Richard's face was more than grim as he addressed his damp and dishevelled wife and son, who had, on his orders, been directed into the morning-room immediately on arrival, without being given time to wash or change.

'It was unforgivable,' he went on. 'The entire household has been worrying over you.'

They stood side by side in front of him like an errant brother and sister being chided by their father for some more than trivial offence. James licked his lips, and said, 'I'm sorry, Father. It was all my fault. I shouldn't have attempted Southwold when the cloud started. Then the fog came down so suddenly, and my compass let me down, too. I'm sorry.'

Richard had made no move to kiss or comfort Virginia when they had come in. His rage had to be vented first. Now, though, she ran to him, and he was holding her tight and saying, 'Oh, my darling, I'm sorry. I shouldn't have shouted at you. You're not hurt, are you – either of you?'

She lifted her tear-stained face.

'No, we're not hurt. But you are, and I need your forgiveness. I did a childish, impetuous thing, trying to show my independence, I suppose. I'm deeply sorry, Richard, for all the fuss and worry I've caused you and the servants.'

'You must blame me, Father,' James intervened. 'I egged her on to come. She got caught up in my enthusiasm, that's all.'

Richard at last gave his little smile with one corner of his mouth.

'Well, these things happen, don't they? I suggest we forget the whole thing and thank God you're back. Suppose you go and get cleaned up and changed. I've ordered luncheon at two.'

James nodded and turned away. 'By the way, my aeroplane's only slightly damaged,' he said. 'It will fly again.'

Richard forebore to comment as James went out. Virginia remained in his arms.

'Promise you're not angry any more,' she pleaded up into his eyes.

'My anger was born of sheer blinding fear, my dear,' he said. 'Ever seen a mother thrash her child for running into the road? All that matters now is that I've got you both back — the two people who matter most to me in all the world.'

His smile broadened and he added softly, 'Damn you!'

She nestled her head against him and he stroked her hair.

CHAPTER FOUR

THE younger female servants, except Lily, who was away on her holidays, were frowning over close-work in the servants' hall. The table was a jumble of items of small boy's clothing.

Daisy was sewing Cash's name tapes on to the soft garments. Ruby, her concentration – for want of a better word – fully engaged, painfully lettered the name WILLIAM HAMILTON and the number 48 on the insides of canvas shoes. The tongue which protruded between her lips was empurpled from licking the point of the indelible pencil.

'Fancy,' she said, withdrawing the tongue and grimacing at the taste: 'Master William having a school number. It's like going to prison.'

'And all these labels,' Dasily grumbled.

Mrs. Bridges sat apart in state. She glanced up from her magazine.

'You're lucky. Aren't they, Rose? Remember when the Major went away to his school? No fancy shop-made labels in them days.'

'Yeh,' Rose agreed. 'Every blessed initial to be sewn by hand. I was kept at it for weeks, even with that woman who came in special to help.'

Daisy sighed. 'One day, Ed and I'll have a nice little boy like William.'

Mr. Hudson had entered in time to overhear this hopeful utterance.

'Time enough for that when you get a bit more put away, Daisy. After what occurred last time.'

Daisy protested, 'We're putting something away in the Post Office Savings every week. 'Sides, it wasn't our fault last time. I mean, it was everyone the same. Government said it was a country fit for heroes, and then wouldn't give us no work . . .'

70

No one answered. It had become a familiar refrain from Daisy since her return to security.

Ruby sighed gustily. 'I wish I could have a little kiddy to send to school.'

Mrs. Bridges and Hudson exchanged a quick and meaningful glance.

'You're well off where you are, Ruby,' Mrs. Bridges told her. 'Remember what happened when *you* went off last time. You got blown up.'

'And you're not even married yet,' Daisy couldn't forbear to add.

Ruby grimaced. 'And it says in t' papers there's a shortage of men . . .'

The tongue emerged again, moistened the purple pencil tip, and she bent to the task of etching an unsymmetrical M.

That evening, James's old school trunk and tuck box, both re-lettered WILLIAM HAMILTON, had been packed, with every last item carefully placed by Rose, assisted, as tally clerk, by Alice. Then Rose withdrew, leaving the children washed and bedded and reading their books, until Virginia came in, dressed for dinner, to kiss them goodnight. The usual requests for time to read 'just one more page' having been turned down, she reminded them of their prayers. Both dutifully got out of bed and knelt. Alice, as always, prayed silently; William, out loud.

'God bless Mummy and Alice . . . and Uncle Richard, and . . . and Aunt Georgina, and Uncle James . . . and Rose and Mrs. Bridges and Mr. Hudson and . . . and everyone else downstairs . . .' He made his usual pause before adding, 'And Daddy and Michael, in Heaven.'

He was getting up, when Virginia reminded him, ' "And Miss Treadwell".'

'Oh, lor',' he groaned, subsiding briefly. 'And Miss Treadwell.' He scrambled up and into bed. Virginia sat on the coverlet.

'Darling, you must promise to go on saying your prayers every night at school.'

'Yes, Mummy. Can I say them in bed?'

'Unless the other boys kneel. Do what they do.'

She picked up the Teddy Bear nestling beside him and regarded its worn countenance, so long taken for granted, with new awareness.

'Perhaps . . . it would be best not to take Edward to school.'

It was the end of something in the lives of mother, child and toy bear.

'Yes, Mummy,' William said. 'I suppose it would.'

'He'll be all right here – waiting for you when you come home.'

There was a knock at the door.

'Yes, Rose,' Virginia called. 'All right.'

Both children stared as Rose entered, wondering how their mother had known it was she who had knocked. Rose was smirking.

'Rose has a surprise for you both,' their mother said. 'Are you ready, Rose?'

'Yes, m'lady. If the children will put on their dressing-gowns and slippers . . .'

It was no sooner requested than done. Rose led all three to her own room. She pushed open the door and stood aside for them to go in.

Blinking in the electric light was a small, brown, long-haired dog, sitting up on its forelegs in a wicker basket.

The children gaped vocally.

'It's to keep Miss Alice company while you're away, Master William,' Rose explained in a rush. 'Of course, it's yours too, though. You remember that day when we was in the park, and you said you wished you could have a dog . . .'

They ran to pet the little animal, which writhed and rolled appreciatively.

'Oh, darling doggie!' Alice exclaimed. 'But aren't you thin! Lots of lovely dinners . . .'

'Thanks so much, Rose,' William said, going to give her a kiss. 'Mummy, can we show him to Treadie, please?'

Virginia nodded. 'I have to go down, darlings. Rose will see you to bed again. Not too long, now.'

They kissed her and she went away, her long dress caught up in one hand. Alice scooped up the dog before William could beat her to it. 'You can carry the basket,' she condescended.

Miss Treadwell was reading in the schoolroom. She looked up, frowning, when the door burst open without a knock and the voices of her two charges cried, excitedly and simultaneously, 'Look what Rose has given us, Miss Treadwell!'

'A dog,' William added superfluously.

The governess stood up, wrinkling her nose. 'I can see that, without having it thrust in my face.'

Rose came forward from the landing. 'Her ladyship said it would be all right, seeing as Master William was going to school.'

'Did she? Is it house-trained?'

'Oh, yes. It said on the notice I saw in a shop in Pont Street. "A well trained dog, ten months, wanting a nice home," 'cos the people was going to Canada.'

'What shall we call it, Rose?' Alice asked.

'Oh, he's got a name already, Miss Alice. He's Thimble.'

'Thimble! Darling Thimble! Oh, what a perfect, divine name!'

Rose looked from the children to Miss Treadwell: clearly, she was not amused.

The painful moment of William's departure had come and gone. He had gone bravely, smart in his new grey flannel suit, in a trouser pocket of which reposed a half-guinea piece, slipped to him by Richard at the last moment: it was the most valuable coin the child had ever possessed.

Grave handshakes for all the staff ('Proper little gentleman; he really is,' Daisy had declared afterwards); but for Rose, a fierce hug and a warm kiss, which had made the watching Miss Treadwell's lips tighten. Then Edward had driven the car away, and in a moment it was out of sight.

Hudson closed the front door, and a pall of anti-climax fell upon upstairs and downstairs, as everyone resumed his or her activity, a little sadder and quieter than before.

The ex-diplomatist in Richard had ensured that he should have a plan ready by which to divert his wife's thoughts. Meeting him in the hall a few days previously as he returned from the House of Lords, she had looked with concern at the lines of tiredness in his face and begged him to take things more easily. He shook his head.

'I went to see Dr. Foley only this morning. Everything's fine. Just getting old, that's all.'

She led him by the arm into the morning-room and poured him a whisky and soda.

'Mind you,' he confessed, 'would you forgive me if I didn't change for dinner?'

She was already changed, but she shook her head emphatically.

'Of course I wouldn't. It's almost ready, anyway, and there's a cheese *soufflé* first. If you were late it could turn out a disaster and I'd have Mrs. Bridges to reckon with.'

'I might have Hudson to reckon with if I don't change,' he answered with his wry smile. 'Ten years ago I wouldn't even have dreamed of it. He'll think I'm getting slack and slovenly.'

'You're just tired, and he can think what he likes. Darling, I really do think you ought to get out of this French trip.'

'Oh, not possible. The King and Queen are going, and I'm on the War Graves Committee.'

His cue had come to enact his plan, and he took it.

'I've just had a splendid idea, though. I'm going to take you with me.'

'Oh, darling!'

'Yes. And afterwards we'll go on to Baden Baden for a week's rest, and then to the Martels, near Aix. They're absolute old darlings, and they never stop asking us.'

'Well, I suppose with William gone it would be a good idea to be out of the house to let the servants do the spring cleaning. What about poor Alice, though?'

'Oh, Miss Treadwell and the others will look after her. They'll all spoil her like anything, you'll see.'

The door opened and Hudson entered. He viewed Richard with open surprise, though it was Virginia he addressed.

'Er, pardon me, m'lady . . . are you and his lordship ready for dinner?'

'Quite ready, thank you, Hudson,' Virginia said, amused by the unspoken criticism, but not showing it.

'In er, that case, m'lady . . . dinner is served.'

And so, William having departed, the eve of Richard and Virginia's own going had been reached. In the schoolroom, Virginia conducted her final interview with Miss Treadwell; or rather, Miss Treadwell conducted the final interview with her.

'The novelty of it is quite exciting at first,' she remarked of the brave face William had worn on leaving home. 'I usually find the second term is the worst, especially for boys.'

Dampened, Virginia said, 'I hope Alice will be all right.'

'I am sure she will. Alice is by no means a stupid girl, but she finds it difficult to concentrate. I think it will be easier for her with William away. We can do proper school hours and evening homework.'

Virginia made the best of things.

'Miss Treadwell, it is such a relief for my husband and myself to be able to go away leaving Alice – indeed, the whole household – in such capable hands.'

'Thank you, Lady Bellamy.' Miss Treadwell gave one of her rare, thin smiles. 'I hope it will be understood by everyone in the house, including the butler, that I am responsible in your absence.'

'Oh yes. I shall make that quite clear.'

'Thank you. I only hope the dog will not prove another, er, disruptive influence.'

'I'm sure not. Rose is willing to look after him during school hours.'

Miss Treadwell made no reply. After a few more words on practical matters Virginia left her, to go downstairs. As she was about to pass William's bedroom she paused, opened the door, and switched on the light. It looked so neat, so tidy, so . . . empty. She went in. Edward Bear was sitting on the chest of drawers, his glass eyes unusually devoid of their make-believe life. Impulsively, Virginia picked him up and took him to the bed. She turned it down and tucked him in.

A shadow fell across her from the doorway. She turned, to see Richard, in evening dress. He came to her and kissed her tenderly on the cheek. She brushed away a tear.

'It didn't seem so bad when Michael went away to Osborne. But William . . . he seems so small, and defenceless.'

'He'll be all right. He's got good manners and he knows how to get on with people and when to keep his mouth shut. It's the bumptious ones who get into trouble.'

'I know. But . . . why? I mean, the French don't . . .'

Richard seated himself beside her on the bed, his arm around her.

'I don't know why,' he said, 'but we're the only nation in the world that tears the male patrician child from the bosom of his family, to be subjected to cold baths, football and Latin infinitives, at the tender age of eight years.'

He felt Virginia shudder slightly.

'What is it?''

'Just suddenly, I wish we weren't going away.'

'I think it's a jolly good thing we are. Make a change for you. Miss Treadwell's perfectly competent, isn't she?'

'Yes. I think so. I don't like her much.'

'Governesses aren't supposed to be liked, are they? At least she seems a stayer, and that's a rarity in my experience. I can't tell you what a time we had with Elizabeth. Her governess came and went like clockwork mice. Of course, it was mostly Elizabeth's fault. She was a little devil. There was one rather pretty, shy French woman . . . Elizabeth found out that she had a silly crush on me and forced the poor creature to race her down the back stairs on a tin tray and give her free sweets, or she'd give her away to Marjorie.'

Virginia smiled at last.

'Girls are much nastier than boys, Richard. They've much more imagination – but I can't see Alice getting Miss Treadwell racing downstairs on a tin tray. Still, you're right. It's probably quite a good thing we're going away.'

That wasn't how the servants saw it, however.

'Schoolroom, Frederick,' Daisy said, as the bell rang, yet again. It was two days after Lord and Lady Bellamy had left. To those below stairs, it seemed as if their considerate master and mistress had been replaced by some sort of Corporation For The Full-Time Employment Of Servants.

Frederick put aside his pipe and newspaper and went out without a word.

'Whatever can she want now?' Rose speculated, holding wool for Daisy to wind. 'They've had their tea.'

Mrs. Bridges looked up from her magazine.

'Marvellous, the way that boy never complains. The way she has him going up and down them stairs, like an Egyptian slave. If it's been once, it's been twenty times today . . .'

'Now, Mrs. Bridges,' said Mr. Hudson, coming into the servants' hall from his pantry. 'If the governness wants something, that is what the footman is here for. With *Them* all away, there's very little else to occupy him – or any of you, come to that.'

He said it unconvincingly, and made no attempt to rebuke Rose when she threw the wool down on to the table and stalked out.

'She can't keep still, that girl,' Mrs. Bridges said uneasily. 'Fidgety.'

Up in the schoolroom, Miss Treadwell was saying to Alice, who had just kissed Thimble and been licked in return: 'Alice, you must not put your face near that dog. Dogs are dirty. Think of the places they go. And I said that dog was not to be brought into the schoolroom during study hours.'

There was a knock at the door and Frederick came in, his handsome face impassive. He did not speak.

'Frederick,' Miss Treadwell commanded, 'you will take the dog to Rose's room, please.'

'Yes, Miss Treadwell.'

He went to take the animal from Alice. It seemed that she might turn her back on him, holding Thimble tighter in her arms. His expression gave her no hint about what he might do if she did. She thought it prudent to surrender.

The spring cleaning began next day. In all the reception rooms sheets were spread over the furniture and the net curtains taken down for washing. On a trestle table in the morning-room, basins of hot and cold water stood on a sheet, upon which were also strewn the hundreds of crystal drops which had formed one of the chandeliers. As Daisy washed each one in the warm water and then rinsed it in the cold, Rose took it over to give it a first polish and then a little wiping with powder-blue, to give it an extra sparkle after the final brisk rub.

Both heads turned and both pairs of eyes stared astonishedly as the double doors opened and Miss Treadwell entered, followed by an expressionless Frederick carrying a coffee tray. He moved ahead of her and whisked back a dustsheet from a fireside chair. Miss Treadwell seated herself stiffly. Frederick set down the tray and began to pour.

Though each felt her indignation matching the other's, Rose and Daisy remained faithful to their training. They laid down their work and quietly they quitted the room.

'Well! Who's she think she is?' The explosion came outside, in the hall, from Daisy. Rose remained silent, white-faced and tight-lipped, until Frederick emerged, closing the doors behind him. Their challenge needed no words to convey it. He shrugged, and told them, 'It's not my place to disobey orders.'

Mr. Hudson supported him, in the servants' hall, a few angry moments later.

'She asked Frederick to serve her coffee in the morning-room, and Frederick consulted me. I could see no reasonable grounds for refusing her request. Miss Treadwell is the governess in this house, and before she left the mistress asked me to do my best to see that she was comfortable.'

'All right for her to be comfortable!' Rose flared. 'Whoever heard of a governess being served coffee in the morning-room? Anyway, couldn't the little cow see we was working in there?'

'Rose!' Mr. Hudson admonished, though with less than complete conviction. 'I am sure Miss Treadwell has two eyes in her head, the same as everyone else. Could . . . you not find some other occupation in the meantime?'

'I tell you, Mr. Hudson,' Rose threatened between her teeth; 'if her ladyship was here . . .'

He could only reply lamely, 'Her ladyship is not here. So let us please be sensible.' He gesticulated with unhappy authority. 'All of you . . . Mrs. Bridges, Ruby . . . you too, please. I want you to listen. The governess, Miss Treadwell, does not wish Miss Alice to visit the servants' quarters in future.'

He raised his hand to quell a murmur of disapproval; both children had always been welcome below stairs, and only that morning Mrs. Bridges had been teaching Alice to bake tartlets and make Genoese paste.

'In future, when you come upon Miss Alice in the normal course of your duties you will treat her with polite formality, just as you would any other member of the family.'

Rose demanded, 'What's all this in aid of, Mr. Hudson? That's what I'd like to know.'

'And so would I,' Mrs. Bridges pouted.

Before this firing-squad of females, with no hope of rescue by the silent Frederick, Mr. Hudson floundered on, 'It, ah, it appears that Miss Alice has been somewhat backward and inattentive with her work lately. The governess believes that fraternising with the servants has not been, ah, beneficial to her concentration.'

'Piffle!' Rose told him. ' "Fraternising with the servants", indeed! I'm going to treat Miss Alice just like I've always treated her – so there!'

'Oh dear, oh dear,' said Mr. Hudson's oldest and staunch-

79

est ally, Mrs. Bridges, when the hostile meeting had dispersed. 'How long's this going on for, Mr. Hudson?'

He shook his head. 'I don't know, Mrs. Bridges. I really don't know.'

They had not long to wait for the next crisis. Alice had arranged to collect the little dog from Rose's room next morning at eleven, to take him into the park. When that hour came, Miss Treadwell was just ordering her pupil to write out Coleridge's poem *Kubla Khan* four times.

'But it's nearly eleven, Miss Treadwell. I'm to take Thimble to the park.'

'Well, we are not now going to the park, so let this be a lesson to us not to be inattentive.'

'But Miss Treadwell . . . !'

'*And* argumentative!'

Rose was busy and had expected Alice to fetch the dog. Since neither went for him, the result, by the time both did, meeting in the doorway, was that the poor little thing had long since been unable to contain himself. He watched contritely as both mopped away with cloths at the surprisingly large pool, for so small a dog, which he had reluctantly created.

'He must have been bursting,' Rose said pityingly, though with something of a giggle.

'I'm sorry, Rose. Miss Treadwell just wouldn't let me go.'

'Alice!' snapped that lady's voice from behind them. 'Go to the schoolroom at once. At once, please.'

Rose glared malevolently at the figure in the doorway as the child slid past.

'I thought that dog was supposed to be house-trained,' Miss Treadwell said, as she turned and went. Rose made a gesture she would not have resorted to had the child still knelt beside her.

'Bread and water!' Mrs. Bridges exploded when the governess's latest edict reached her as she was finishing preparing that evening's meal. 'I never heard nothing like it. It's like putting the poor child to medieval torture. And

I suppose *she* expects a slap-up dinner in the dining-room.'

Mr. Hudson did his unenthusiastic best to defend the rule of law.

'Miss Treadwell's orders are to be obeyed, Mrs. Bridges. And we do know that Miss Alice can be very wilful and obstinate on occasion.'

'Stuff and nonsense! She's as sweet as a lamb, that child. And clever. It's the way people are treated that counts. Why, she's only a little girl still.'

'When I was her age,' Ruby offered, 'I'd run away from t'mill into service.'

Mrs. Bridges flourished a saucepan under her nose.

'Yes. And from the state of this, it's a pity you didn't stay in the mill.'

'Dried up old bitch!'

They all looked up in astonishment, to see Rose in the doorway, the dog in her arms. Her usually pale cheeks were scarlet and her fine eyes were like polished minerals, flashing with her reflected hate.

'Really, Rose . . .' Mr. Hudson began, but she ignored him.

'I don't care what anyone says. She *is* one – and a witch, too, if you ask me. I love Miss Alice. She's a real darling, and that dried up stick of a woman hates her. She shouldn't be allowed near her, let alone in charge.'

'What is it, Rose?' Mrs. Bridges asked. Even Rose's fury had not burned up her sense of propriety: she put the animal down in the servants' hall, rather than commit the gross sin of bringing him into Mrs. Bridges' kitchen. Then she herself came in and told them of the latest outrage.

'Miss Alice had Thimble in her room for a bit . . . Well, I know she wasn't supposed, but I thought it would calm her after that telling-off. She heard that woman coming and hid him in a cupboard, but she found him. She was going to thrash the poor little animal with a slipper, only Miss Alice pulled her away. Then Miss Treadwell slapped her, and Miss Alice hit her back and scratched her.'

'That was a terrible thing for a child to do to her governness,' Hudson said, genuinely horrified.

Mrs. Bridges added thoughtfully, 'Master William seemed very fond of her. She can't be all that bad . . .'

At that moment, Frederick came in from the servants' hall, to ask, 'Schoolroom supper ready, Mrs. Bridges?'

Mrs. Bridges seemed to make up her mind.

'Yes, it is,' she said firmly. 'Two trays tonight. Bread and water for Miss Alice.' She gestured towards a tray Ruby had already prepared. 'And for Miss Treadwell . . .' Mrs. Bridges picked up a saucepan from the side of the cooker and poured its contents unceremoniously on to a cold plate: '. . . some nice congealed stew.'

They all watched intently as the glutinous mess spread and settled in its own fat. Even the impassive Frederick gulped.

'She won't like it.'

The cook demolished him with a glare. 'You just take it up, and stop answering back.'

'Yes, Mrs. Bridges.'

Miss Treadwell did not like it, and presently summoned Mr. Hudson to the morning-room, where he found her grimacing over a cup of tepid and gritty coffee.

'You wished to see me . . .?' He managed to avoid saying 'Miss' or 'Miss Treadwell'.

'Yes, Hudson, I did. Firstly, it was to ask you to tell Mrs. Bridges that my supper was quite inedible. One would have expected, in a house like this, that something might be properly cooked, even if simple.'

'I will speak to her . . .'

'Now, about the dog. I'm sorry to say I find its presence in this house a distruptive and disturbing influence which cannot go on. I have decided to take it to a veterinary surgeon, to be disposed of in a humane manner.'

For once in his life, Hudson almost stammered.

'I . . . I am sure that Rose could . . . could keep the dog in some safe place . . .'

'On the contrary, I find that Rose has signally failed to look after it, as I was promised she would.'

'I see. But, er, have you mentioned this to Miss Alice...?'

'I think that is hardly your concern, Hudson,' Miss Treadwell said, rejecting the coffee finally. 'Please see that the animal is put into a basket or other receptacle and brought to the hall at ten o'clock tomorrow morning. I shall require a taxicab and the services of the footman to carry the animal. That is all, thank you.'

Shattered, Hudson picked up the coffee tray and went in silence. When he told his news in the kitchen the servants' brief feeling of triumph won for them by Mrs. Bridges was swept away by a flood-tide of dismay, anger, and then rebellion.

At ten o'clock precisely next morning Mr. Hudson entered the hall from the pass door, to find Miss Treadwell standing there, thin and erect in her severe outdoor clothes.

'Well?' she demanded without preamble. 'Where is the dog?'

'I, er, I'm sorry, Miss Treadwell. It appears it has been, er, mislaid.'

She had been half-expecting this. Her look blended anger and disdain.

'You mean it has been deliberately mislaid. Hidden, no doubt.'

'Er, Rose reported to me that...'

'Where is Rose?'

'In the servants' hall... Miss.'

Without hesitation, Miss Treadwell swept past him and through the pass door, down into the hall. The servants were grouped together, apprehensive but defiantly silent as her gaze raked them.

'Hudson, will you please ask the staff the whereabouts of Miss Alice's dog?'

Her eyes had come to rest on Rose. Before Hudson could obey or answer, Rose was saying, 'If you're asking me...'

'Yes, I am asking you, Rose.'

'Very well, *Miss* Treadwell. In the first place, my name isn't Rose. It's *Miss* Buck, so please don't forget it. I'm Lady Bellamy's maid and I don't take orders from nobody else in this household – certainly no governess. And secondly, that dog don't belong to you or me or to anyone else except Miss Alice, and she loves it.'

'Where *is* it?'

'I dunno; and if I did I wouldn't tell you. You're the last person in the world I would tell, because you can't stand seeing people fond of each other, like Miss Alice is fond of Thimble, and I'm fond of her, and she's fond of me. It drives you mad with jealousy, doesn't it?'

'Rose!' Mr. Hudson interjected weakly, but she ignored him, thrusting her face towards Miss Treadwell, as if to give more velocity to her words.

'Poor thing! What hope for you is there in this world?'

The contempt, put in this form, hurt Miss Treadwell, war-widow, keenly; but Miss Treadwell, governess, managed to conceal it. She turned her look upon each servant in turn. They stared her out blankly – all except Ruby, who lacked the resources to do so.

'It . . .' she blurted. 'It run away.'

In the moment of silence which followed there was almost an air of apprehension that Rose would fling herself on Ruby to silence her physically. But there was no need; Miss Treadwell was turning contemptuously away.

'So this is a conspiracy of silence. I hope you are aware of what you are doing, that's all I can say. Lord and Lady Bellamy are returning tomorrow – and then, God help you all.'

They watched silently as she stalked away up the stairs and let the door at their top thud behind her. There was no jubilation at her rout. Mutiny by servants against their officially designated superior was almost as serious a matter as its equivalent on the high seas; and if the penalty were not quite so drastic, the thought of possible dismissal with a bad reference, or no reference at all, was a sobering one.

Even the considerate nature of Lord and Lady Bellamy couldn't be taken for granted.

They went about their duties quietly. Only Frederick, the war survivor who had come unscathed through too much to care overly about the possible outcome of a domestic fracas, moved close to Daisy and whispered, 'After all that, where is it?'

She couldn't help giving a little smirk as she replied, 'In Eddie's and my room, over the garage.'

Later, when they could bring themselves to discuss it, the servants debated whether or not Miss Alice should be told of Thimble's whereabouts. Rose, who had heard the child sobbing, was all for writing a reassuring note and pushing it under the child's door. Mr. Hudson, whom the conspiracy had regarded as merely a watcher-on so far, hastened to deter her.

'I think you would be most unwise, Rose. A child in Miss Alice's state should not be entrusted with secrets. She'll blurt it out and then that . . . that woman will have the dog along at the vet's first thing.'

Rose regarded Hudson with new respect, but said, 'You mean we've got to leave her in ignorance all this time? Thinking maybe he's run away, or something?'

'I tell you, it's the only way, Rose. In fact, if Miss Alice does question you – any of you – you'd better say her dog is missing. The police have been informed and are confident of finding him. Remind her that he has his name and this address on his collar.'

The night held many anxious minutes for most of them, on several accounts. They were not to be kept long in suspense next morning, however, for their master and mistress were due at an early hour off the boat train. Edward drove off to meet them and the bustle of getting the house into final immaculacy made the time go swiftly. At length, the car was at the front door, Frederick was bringing in the many pieces of baggage, and Mr. Hudson and Rose were helping their employers off with their coats. The holiday had clearly done them both good. Lord

Bellamy looked relaxed and younger. Her ladyship, in a Paris-tailored outfit in mauve, with a hat to match, was smiling and positively lovely.

'I trust you had a good trip, m'lord?' Hudson enquired.

'Excellent, thank you,' Richard smiled, allowing himself to give his stomach a meaningful little pat. 'Wonderful food . . . Oh, don't tell Mrs. Bridges I said that!'

Hudson smiled and asked, 'M'lady, will you be requiring breakfast?'

'No thank you. We had it on the boat train. Some coffee would be nice, though, wouldn't it, Richard?'

He had barely had time to nod when a little thunderbolt in white hurtled down the main stairs and into Virginia's arms.

'Oh, Mummy, Mummy!' Alice sobbed.

Surprised at the emotional greeting, Virginia asked, 'Darling? How are you?'

'Terrible! Everything's awful. Come in here.'

She dragged her mother into the morning-room. Richard paused for a questioning glance at Hudson and Rose before going quickly in. The two servants exchanged a look of their own, before Hudson jerked his head and they went below stairs to order the coffee.

Richard Bellamy had never been a man eager to come to grips with the crises of domestic life. When Marjorie had been alive she had been so adept at handling any situation, whether it stemmed from above stairs or below, or both, that he had acquired the habit of leaving her to deal with it, while he shut himself away with his letters, or, in more extreme circumstances, hurried off to his club or suddenly remembered some business needing urgent attention at his office.

Now, he found himself thinking, he had only to step happily back into the house after only a fortnight away, to find himself beset by turmoil at once. Instinctively, he took out his watch, but put it away at once. No possible excuse would do this time. Besides, he was genuinely concerned to know what had upset his stepdaughter to make her cry so bitterly.

86

After some moments her mother succeeded in calming her and persuading her to tell what was the matter.

'Poor . . . poor Thimble's lost and Miss Treadwell's been dreadfully horrid. Rose thinks she's a bit cuckoo, and so do I. And,' the child added, more urgently, to her astonished mother, 'whatever she says, don't believe a word.'

The warning was delivered only just in time, for Hudson had entered. He paused respectfully to gain Virginia's attention before saying, 'The governess would like a word with you, m'lady.'

Richard protested, 'But we've only just come off the train . . .'

But Miss Treadwell was pushing past the butler and into the room. Her thin face was paler than ever and her lips were trembling with agitation as she said, 'This matter is extremely urgent, Lady Bellamy. If you please . . .'

Virginia looked at Richard. He could only shrug.

'All right,' she agreed. 'Alice, darling, you go and help Rose unpack our things.'

'Yes, Mummy,' Alice said, casting a meaningful glance behind her as she went to the door, where Hudson gently ushered her out and followed.

Virginia sat down and gave Miss Treadwell a smile.

'We were so sorry to hear about the dog,' she told the governess, who still stood unsmiling.

Miss Treadwell came close to snorting.

'If you ask me, the servants are hiding it. It's not lost. Not lost at all. It's all part of their plot.'

'Plot?' Richard and Virginia exchanged glances again. Miss Treadwell saw them.

'Oh, I expect Hudson's been telling you a pack of lies about me.'

Richard could be firm when provoked. 'Miss Treadwell, I have known Hudson half my life, and I can assure you he is one of the most honest men I've ever come across.'

Virginia said, more gently, 'What has been the trouble?'

With a rush, the governess let off all the steam which had been building up inside her.

'Every single person in this household has conspired to subvert my authority, Lady Bellamy. The lady's maid has been impertinent and has insulted me to my face in front of the others. The butler has disobeyed my orders and lied to me. The cook has tried to poison me. The footman laughs at me behind my back. In all my experience, I have never known such a disobedient, mutinous pack of servants. No wonder your daughter is such a tiresome, wilful girl when she is allowed to mix with them. She actually struck me, that child. She needs a good beating. And as for that dog . . .'

Her near-hysterical tirade was cut off, not by any reprimand from her amazed employers, but by the sound of the door opening behind her. She stopped and turned to see Frederick carrying the silver tray with the coffee things. Mr. Hudson entered the room with him and deftly helped him set out the pieces.

'There is good news about the dog, m'lady,' Hudson said blandly, as though unaware of the tension in the air. 'It has been found in the mews.'

His smile took in Miss Treadwell as he turned to follow Frederick out of the room. The governess was beside herself.

'There! What did I tell you, Lady Bellamy? The second you get back, the dog is miraculously found. And the sooner it is got rid of and put to sleep, the better . . .'

'Put to sleep!'

'It is a dirty, destructive animal. Half the trouble in this place has been caused by that dog. As I said at the time . . .'

Virginia's expression was anything but smiling now as she cut in briskly, 'Miss Treadwell, it sounds to me that you would be happier away from here.'

'I can assure you, I wouldn't have stayed another minute in this miserable house but for a sense of loyalty to you and Lord Bellamy.'

'That is very loyal of you. Well, we are back now, so you

needn't worry any further. May I suggest two weeks' wages in lieu of notice?'

A flush which had risen to Miss Treadwell's cheeks with her outburst deepened swiftly.

'So I'm to be thrown out, like a . . . a . . .'

Richard reminded her, 'But you yourself suggested . . .'

She interrupted rudely, 'I suggest you get rid of Rose and that . . . that butler, and then perhaps you might get some control over your own daughter.'

'I think that's up to us to decide,' Virginia snapped back.

'Oh, yes! I knew you wouldn't listen to me. You never do, you sort of people. No wonder your servants run riot the moment your back is . . .'

'Miss Treadwell!' Richard stopped her. Even in her rage she knew better than to go on.

'Very well. I know when I'm not wanted. I'll go with pleasure. *Four* weeks' *salary* it should be, if you look at the usual terms of employment as laid down by the agencies.'

She turned swiftly and went. When the door had shut Richard groaned aloud and began to pour the coffee.

Virginia said, 'Oh dear! I really think she is rather mad. I do hate rows. I wonder if I've enough money to pay her, without going to the bank.'

He got out his wallet and peered in.

'How much a week?'

'One pound ten.'

Richard fingered notes. 'Yes, I can manage.'

He sighed inwardly. In the absence of the complete freedom of being away on holiday, the hurly-burly of politics and his clubs seemed so inviting, compared with domesticity. It was a pity. He'd known so much happiness in this home. A good deal of sorrow and strife, too, but happy memories predominated. It was the niggling, tiresome little incidents such as this which seemed to drain one so.

He wondered passingly what it would be like to live without servants. Simply exchanging one lot of problems for another, he was sure. In any case, such a notion was as unthinkable as another world war.

Virginia felt suddenly deflated, too. After drinking the coffee and glancing through a few letters she went slowly up to her room, where she found Rose and Alice putting her things into piles for washing, sending to the laundry, and other purposes. The smiles with which both greeted her lifted her spirits a little.

Rose managed to whisper, briefly out of the child's earshot, 'I hope you don't think I deliberately disobeyed Miss Treadwell, m'lady.'

Virginia shook her head. 'Of course not, Rose.'

'If I did, it was for Miss Alice's sake – and for poor Thimble.'

Alice came and clung to her mother.

'Mummy, when Miss Treadwell's gone, need I have another governess?'

'I don't think so, dear. Uncle Richard and I have just had a word or two about it. He thinks it would be best if you went to a day school.'

'Oh, yes please, Mummy! Horrible old ...'

Virginia stopped her firmly.

'That's enough, now.' She changed her tone deliberately. 'I've had a letter from William. Here you are.'

Alice took it eagerly. 'Listen, Rose,' she commanded, and read out carefully: 'Dear Mummy, I hope you are well. I am very well. We had a lecher – he means lecture, silly – about lifeboats it was very good. I am in dorm. B. Must stop now. Lots of love to everyone including Treadie and Thimble.'

She handed the letter back with a smile.

'Well, William loved her, anyway. I suppose that's something.'

CHAPTER FIVE

MR. HUDSON, Mrs. Bridges and Daisy watched, with varying
expressions of curiosity and trepidation, as Edward gestured
to Lily, positioning her exactly where he wanted her a few
feet away from the servants' hall table, round which the
others were gathered. In her hand she held a short, wand-
like piece of metal, connected by a wire to the box of
gadgetry on the table.

'Just there, Lily. Now, hold perfectly still.'

'That looks very dangerous, Edward,' Mr. Hudson said.
'Are you sure you know what you're doing?'

Edward nodded, intent upon connecting two more wires
from the box to the lower end of a metal horn, fluted at its
mouth like an open flower and clearly descended in design
from the long-familiar gramophone horn.

'It's all right, Mr. Hudson. It's just an aerial. There's no
electricity going through it. Now, all we have to do is
connect the terminals to the battery . . . Now, to switch
on . . .'

He turned one of the knobs protruding from the side of
the box. There was no explosion, no movement, no sound –
nothing at all.

Mrs. Bridges snorted. 'Just as I thought.'

'It's got to warm up,' Edward told her. 'Just wait and
see.'

And in a few moments a pink glow was appearing in
each of the two valves on the box's top. Faintly, then louder,
there came from the horn the moans and crackles of
'atmosphere', to give way at last to the tinny sound of a
soprano voice warbling an operatic aria to piano ac-
companiment.

Edward looked round the others proudly.

'There you are – Station 2LO of the British Broadcasting

Company, Savoy Hill. Been broadcasting every day since last November.'

'Isn't it beautiful music?' Daisy said, wide-eyed.

'More like a parrot squawking, if you ask me,' Mrs. Bridges said. 'Where's it coming from, anyway? Them bulbs?'

'Valves, Mrs. B,' Edward corrected. 'It's coming through the air, in waves.'

'Through the air? If you expect me to believe that that voice is coming here from Savoy Hill, all through the traffic and the houses and that . . . *And* with the window closed! How can waves of air get through solid glass? Answer me that one.'

Lily tried, 'Perhaps they're getting through that crack under the back door.'

The song ended and a male announcer's voice was heard.

'And now to the Sporting News. The Football Association Cup Final this year will be held at the new Wembley Stadium and will be between Bolton Wanderers and West Ham United . . .'

'Switch off the apparatus, please, Edward,' Mr. Hudson requested. 'West Ham should never have reached Wembley.'

'Oh, no, Mr. Hudson!' Daisy was protesting, but it was not objection to the content of the news that had motivated him. He alone had heard a taxicab stopping outside the house and anticipated the ringing of the front door bell, which now occurred.

'That will be the Major returning. Now, do as I say, please.'

Edward obeyed, and Mr. Hudson went away up the stairs.

'Out again, was he?' Mrs. Bridges said, shaking her head. 'Poor lonely soul. I wonder what he does?'

'Goes to his club, I reckon,' Daisy answered. 'Or one of them. He belongs to dozens.'

Edward corrected his wife. 'Most likely the Hot Cat Club in Gerrard Street, these nights. His evening things don't half stink of scent.'

It had, indeed, been the Hot Cat Club; as it was again the following evening. James's restlessness was increasing. As each new attempt at diminishing it failed, it was as if it fed upon that failure, and grew. His foray into politics had got him nowhere. The sudden preoccupation with flying had only forced-landed him into trouble. Now, feeling himself virtually incapable of positive effort, he had taken to mooning about the house or his gentlemen's clubs for most of the day, then a taxi to the Hot Cat in the evenings, there to dance and drink with any girl who would share his table and his bottle and his dance-floor embrace for the going rate of payment.

Now, on this spring evening of 1923, he was dancing again with a girl who had partnered him several times before – a respectable young war orphan who had taken the job at a friend's urging in order to escape the tumult of the apartment she shared with two other girls from the whole-sale clothing store in which she worked by day. They had little to say to one another: the tired girl going through the paid motions, the listless James unsuccessfully seeking however little of that increasingly elusive quality, pleasure.

On one or two of their encounters he had wondered whether it would be worth asking the girl to go to bed with him. She didn't seem the promiscuous type, but perhaps she would agree. He could no doubt persuade her to accept some sort of present which would not leave her feeling she had prostituted herself.

He was thinking such a thought again this evening. But, as always, the problems seemed insuperable. He couldn't ask her to take him back to her small shared room. He couldn't take her to Eaton Place. There were no rooms on the premises of the Hot Cat Club. The only remaining alternative was to hire a short-time room in some back-street hotel, a notion which filled James with revulsion as he pictured the receptionist's studied nonchalance, to be followed by a leer at the girl when James's back was turned.

Yet again, he abandoned the idea, and wondered, as the

dance ended, whether to retain the girl. As he hesitated, and she waited to see whether he would lead her to a table, he heard laughter and saw a party of young people, dressed in evening clothes, coming down the stairs. He recognised them, and saw amongst them the kittenishly beautiful Diana Newbury, the young wife of his friend, the Marquis, who, he noticed with interest, was not one of the party.

James turned to his partner and gave her a quick, friendly smile.

'Make yourself scarce, there's a good girl, eh?' he asked. She recognised the situation, smiled back, and went away without rancour.

She had barely left his side when Diana came skipping across. She was dressed in up-to-the-minute butterfly-wing colours, her brown hair modishly fringed and bobbed, her huge eyes glittering with vivacity.

'James! How marvellous! I'm not interrupting anything, am I?'

'Lord, no. I'm here by myself,' he only half-lied. 'How splendid to see you, Diana. I say, do sit down.'

'No. You come over and join us. You know them all – Christabel, Mouse, Davina . . .'

He shook his head. 'I don't think I will, if you don't mind. Diana, do have a drink with me. Please.'

Puzzled, she nodded and joined him at a small table, waving to the others to carry on without her. James was lucky to catch a passing waiter. He ordered two Sidecars.

'What are you doing here, all alone?' she asked.

'Well, something to do, you know. Father and Virginia and the children are still up in Scotland. Georgina's visiting Elizabeth and her husband in America. The house is so damned quiet. Anyway, I like the pianist here. Have you heard him?'

'Not yet. That's why Davina suggested we come tonight. Do join us, James. You shouldn't be alone.'

The drinks came. They touched glasses and sipped the cocktail. James left her invitation unanswered and made no move to get up.

94

'Had a good season?' he asked.

She shrugged and pouted. 'I suppose so. I'm rather bored with hunting, and the country. Everyone endlessly moaning about the miseries of farming.'

'Where are you going to live in London? I see Bunny's selling Newbury House.'

'Thank heavens. It's a dreadful old barrack, really. They're going to pull it down and build a big block of luxury flats. We're supposed to have the best one, at the top overlooking Hyde Park. As a matter of fact, I'm meant to be looking after moving everything out, but I'm staying at the Ritz and just buying new clothes. It's a lovely change.'

She gave the brilliant smile in which every part of her features played its share. James said, 'Where is Bunny?'

'Somewhere in the wilds of Wales. Fishing.' She grimaced. 'He never comes to London, unless it's for a meeting or a dinner. But then, you never come to see us in the country these days.'

'That's true.'

'Not for want of asking, you know.'

'No.'

'No Hazel to hold you back any more.'

'No. Poor Hazel.'

'Does she haunt you from the grave?' she asked mercilessly, despite the smile. She had never hidden her contempt for his seemingly joyless wife and her suburban background.

'Not at all,' he said without resentment. 'My memories of her are happy ones. Happier than when she was alive, I'm afraid.'

Diana said suddenly, 'What are you doing this weekend?'

'Going down to Sandwich for a week or so, to play some golf. The Danbys have lent me their cottage.'

'Who with?'

'By myself.'

'Can I come, too?'

It was said with a casual directness that was entirely typical of Diana. She always said what came into her mind, and anything she impulsively wanted she asked for, without qualification.

For the first time for days James felt a little leap of excitement inside him. She was adding, 'That's if you'd like me to.'

He said carefully, 'It would be . . . rather risky.'

'Why? My maid's absolutely all right.'

He considered. 'So's my man, I suppose.'

'Good, then.'

And that was that. Diana informed him that she would make her own way down, with her maid, by train and go straight to the cottage, which she knew. She finished her drink; leaned over and kissed him; and went gaily away to rejoin her friends. James paid his bill and went straight home.

Two days later found him in the Danbys' cottage in the delightful, half-timbered little Kentish town. Gothic windows looked on to a small, well kept lawn and walled flower garden. The interior furnishings were simple but had cost money.

James heard Edward, who had driven him down, tinkering with something in the small kitchen. He went through and found him priming an oil lamp.

'Just testing it, sir,' Edward explained. 'In case the electricity goes, like last time.'

'Just like the war,' James said. He could hear an edge of nervousness on his voice which reminded him of some wartime moments. 'Er, Edward . . . you know I mentioned the possibility of . . . of a visitor . . .'

'Yes, sir. I've made up the spare bed.'

'Oh, good. There may also be a servant. A maid.'

'There isn't any other room, sir. I could try in the town for her . . .'

'No, no.'

'Well . . . I could make a bed up for myself on the settee in the lounge, if you don't mind. Then she can have my room.'

'Good idea. Thanks. Er, it may not be necessary, but . . .

Anyway, I'm sure the maid will be a help . . . give you a hand.'

'Yes, sir.'

James said deliberately, 'I know I can rely on your discretion, Edward.'

His servant's expression didn't change.

'Yes, sir.'

James relaxed. 'Splendid. They should be here any time now.'

As if on cue, they did arrive, before Edward could offer to take the car and meet them at the station, which would have been unnecessary, anyway, for it was only two minutes' walk away. He answered the doorbell and recognised Lady Newbury at once, and thought how smashing she looked in her checked coat with leopard-skin trimmings.

'Oh, good afternoon, m'lady. Major Bellamy is in here.'

He gestured across the short passage to the open living-room door. There was no space to move to announce her. She gave him a radiant smile and went in.

Edward turned to see the maid waiting just inside the cottage door. A smart piece, too, he noticed approvingly: young, nice figure, bright blonde hair, nicely made-up.

'Hullo,' he grinned. 'My name's Barnes – like the bridge.'

'Mine's Marshall. How d'ye do?'

'Here, let me.' He took the suitcases and went first with them up the narrow stairs.

In the living-room, James and Diana stood back from their kiss and she wandered over to the smouldering fire in the ample grate.

'Some sherry?' he suggested.

'What I'd really like is some gin. Gin and water.'

He poured. 'I thought we might go out to lunch. There are several quite respectable pubs.'

'I've brought some cold food. It would be rather more sensible to eat here, wouldn't it?'

James took her meaning. 'I suppose it would.' He passed over her glass. 'Sorry the fire's rather smoky. Wet wood, I expect.'

They saluted one another silently and drank.

'Well,' James said, 'you're here.'

She wandered over to the sofa and sat. 'Didn't you think I'd come?'

'Well . . .'

'I always do what I say I'll do – you should know that. Aren't you going to say you're glad to see me?'

He quickly went to bend over and kiss her again before joining her on the sofa, leaving a respectable little space between them.

'Of course I am. Tremendously glad. Diana, it's just . . .'

'Just what?'

'Well, Bunny.'

She looked cross suddenly. 'Look, if you've suddenly developed a conscience, why the hell didn't you tell me not to come?'

'I haven't.'

'Right. So let's get it quite clear – no more Bunny.' The smile returned. 'And I've just realised I'm starving.'

James went to the bell. Edward, who had just regained the kitchen, hurried in to answer it, instinctively pausing to knock first.

'Oh, er, Edward,' James said, 'do you think you could rustle up a spot of lunch? Lady Newbury's brought some things. On a tray will do.'

'And a bottle of Burgundy,' Diana put in.

'Yes, sir, m'lady.'

When Edward had gone, Diana said, 'What a nice, willing boy.'

'Yes,' James agreed. 'He's a jolly good fellow.'

'My girl's a bolshie little stuck-up bitch,' she went on. 'The way she behaves, you'd think she was the Queen of Sheba.'

'Why d'you keep her?'

'Oh, she can sew. She's brilliant with hair. And she makes me laugh. You know, your Edward would make someone a very good butler.'

'Diana, you're scheming.'

'Me? Never.'

'You are. Behind that pretty, innocent little face of yours there's a cunning, devious brain.'

Without tilting her head she glanced upwards and at him and smiled enigmatically. He found all thoughts of Bunny receding fast.

In the kitchen, Edward and the 'bolshie little stuck-up bitch' worked side by side to prepare the luncheon of Harrods' comestibles, fresh that morning.

'Lucky we brought our own food,' she said. 'To judge by the look of the larder.'

'The Major usually eats out,' Edward defended.

'I wasn't thinking of them. Poky little place, isn't it?'

'Quite cosy, really. I mean, it's not what we're used to . . .'

'It's not what *we're* used to either, I can assure you, Mr. Barnes. Still, in the circumstances . . .'

'Yeh. You know, you could have knocked me down with a feather when I saw who it was. I mean, I've known Lady Newbury for years. I've been up at Somerby with the Major for the hunting. That was before your time, of course, Miss Marshall. Yeh, you could've knocked me down with a feather.'

'Men are all the same, Mr. Barnes.'

'But I . . . I always understood the Marquis was one of the Major's best friends.'

'What's that got to do with it?'

He jerked his head towards the living-room. 'Well, you know.'

'I think you sound old fashioned, Mr. Barnes . . . Or is it that you've led a sheltered life?'

'No I haven't, not really. I'm married – to Daisy, our head housemaid. And I've been all through the war.'

'I'm glad.'

'About the war?'

'No, the other. I much prefer valets who know what's what. As we seem to have to keep each other company quite a bit, you may call me Violet.'

'Ta. I'm Edward.'

99

'Edward. That's quite nice. Ready?'

They carried a tray each into the living-room. Once again, Edward paused to knock and waited to be called.

Early that afternoon he put aside the washing-up things and went to answer the living-room bell. This time he went straight in.

'Edward,' said Violet Marshall from the sofa in a languid tone, 'you may pour me a glass of Crème de Menthe.'

'Yes, m'lady,' he said, playing up to her.

'Go on, boy, hurry,' she ordered, and got up to go to the gramophone.

'Here, you're going it a bit, aren't you?' Edward said, as the quick strains of 'I'm Just Wild About Harry' burst out and Violet launched into an abandoned dance.

'They're playing golf,' she said, dancing on. 'Won't be back for hours.'

'Here,' he said with genuine admiration, 'you can't half dance.'

'That's what Noël said to me, dahling,' she replied, and after a few more steps flung herself back on to the sofa. Edward sat nearby.

'Where did you learn?'

The mimicking voice continued: 'I picked up that step at Deauville, last season, dahling. A fancy dress ball at the Casino. Everybody was there – the Aga Khan, Gaby Deslys, the Prince of Wales, wrapped round Mrs. Dudley Ward, of course. The King of Sweden winked at me. Elsa Maxwell asked me to one of her parties. A baron asked me to marry him. It was all so terribly gay and boring.'

She dropped the accent and said, not quite in her own voice, 'I think I'll have a bath. Run up and turn it on for me, there's a pet.'

'Here, who d'you think I am?'

'You are quite a dear boy, that's what I think you are. At home I have a footman who is madly in love with me enough to obey my slightest whim. Here, I've only got you.'

Edward got up, grinning. 'Oh, all right.'

'Oh, and Edward . . . don't forget a hot water bottle for my bed. It's bound to be damp.'

She winked and popped into her mouth a chocolate from an open box on the low table beside her. Edward went off, telling himself he might have to watch that one, before the week was out.

'Why did you come down here, Diana?' James asked, two evenings later.

He had been nerving himself to ask it for hours, but had been more than half-afraid to hear what her answer would be. Now he had to.

The fire, unextinguished since it had first been lit, was now well established in a steady, soothing glow. The curtains were drawn against the world; a single electric table lamp gave light but no glare, and the shadows softened the planes and angles of the walls.

James sat on the sofa, looking down at Diana who was on the floor, leaning against his legs. Warmth, comfort and relaxation after a good meal made the asking of a frank question a safer proposition than at some other times.

'Not for a naughty weekend,' she answered. She turned her head to look up at him. 'You silly old thing, it's because I love you.'

She smiled to see his eyebrows go up, but went on, half-flippantly, 'I've loved you ever since an awful dance at Crewe House. I mean awful, because I was thirteen and had spots and was the scourge of many governesses, and you were still at Eton, tall and slim and beautiful. And because our parents knew each other, you actually danced with me, out of duty, because you were properly brought up.'

James smiled. 'Did I?'

She went on, the flippancy left behind. 'And I fell in love with you. And when I found myself in your arms all last night and the night before, I was feeling that same pang. And now that you haven't a wife any more . . . well, I'm yours, if you'll have me.'

'Well . . .' he hesitated, wondering how to answer.

'Well?' she challenged.

He took the risk he had to take. 'Why did you marry Bunny?'

There was no flare-up this time.

'You should know very well, I agreed to marry him in a fit of pique. Old Lady Newbury asked me to stay at Somerby because she thought I would make a more suitable marchioness than the chorus girls Bunny was running after at the time. I really went there because I knew you were going to be there. And when you didn't pop the question, I just said "yes" to poor old Bunny, who'd been asking me dutifully twice daily after meals. Of course, I didn't know then about Hazel and her bewitching middle-class magic. It's taken me a long time to run you to ground, James.'

'I'm sure Bunny's always been kind to you.'

'Of course he has. Always considerate and thoughtful, even when I've been at my most bloody. Life at Somerby is so dull and organised and . . . and *decent*. There's no spice in it; no adventure; no risk. I'm just part of the furniture, beautifully looked after, polished daily. And Bunny's so . . . wet.'

'He did jolly well in the war.'

'He was an A.D.C. most of the time.'

'Only the last year, when most of the heirs of the nobility had been killed and the King wanted to be sure there would still be a House of Lords in the future.'

She frowned. 'Anyway, why are we talking about Bunny again?'

'Well, he is rather germane to the issue, as they say. He is your husband and one of my oldest friends. Don't you think he'd be terribly upset if you just left him for me?'

'I don't think he'll mind, once he's got over the first shock. In fact, I should say he'll be secretly rather relieved. And his family will be delighted that he'll be free to marry again and find a girl who can produce an heir.'

James got up uneasily, walked ruminatively about, then stooped from his great height to kiss her, before moving away to lean against the mantelpiece and gaze into the fire.

'I wish I could see into the future,' he confessed. 'Diana the enchantress. How I chose Hazel, when I could have had you . . . You know, we'd be outcasts. Bunny has thousands of friends and they'll most of them be bound to side with him.'

'Nice to know who one's own friends really are.'

'And you might be in for rather a shock. I know divorce is becoming a commonplace sort of thing nowadays . . . but not among marquises. The King and Queen won't like it a bit.'

'Trying to frighten me?'

'Yes.'

'You've picked the wrong girl.'

He sighed expressively. 'What do you want to do?'

'Go and live abroad. We've both got a bit of money. Let's spend it. We could live in Paris, hunt with Bendor Westminster's hounds at Pau . . . Brioni for the polo . . . and we could rent a villa with a wild romantic old garden at Fiesole. There'd be parties all the time – skiing parties in the Alps, yachting parties in Greece, mad gondolier parties in Venice, bathing parties at Monte. We'll go everywhere and do everything. There's nothing we couldn't do together.'

The infection of her enthusiasm had found a susceptible subject. Pushing his misgivings firmly to the back of his mind, James raised her to her feet, and, his arm round her, led her away up the stairs.

They heard little of the rain which started soon afterwards and continued through most of the night. But in the morning the lowering wet sky, the soaked garden, and the dank smell of renewed dampness throughout the cottage did nothing for their spirits. Mah Jong, which James persuaded Diana to try, was soon pronounced boring, complicated and silly. Bezique was rejected as being fit only for dowagers. Rain sputtered down the old chimney on to the fire, making it black and smoky.

'Darling, please don't light another of those cigars,' Diana said irritably. 'The whole place stinks of them already.'

He put it back in the box. 'All right, darling. What about a walk? Bit of exercise, fresh air . . .'

'In this weather?'

There was no pleasing her. He went to the window, to peer out at the downpour and wonder what to suggest next. The initiative came from her.

'James, darling . . .'

'Mm?'

'Why don't we go and look for the sun?'

He turned, surprised. 'Now? Where?'

'France. We've got your car. I've got plenty of money on me. There's the ferry from Dover. We could just nip across.'

'Well . . . it's a bit . . . sudden, isn't it? We can't just up sticks and . . .'

She came over to stand in front of him, looking directly into his eyes, her own flashing an unmistakable challenge.

'Why not, James?'

He couldn't answer.

She smiled. 'I think we should pack.'

Mrs. Bridges' eyes widened at what she had just read in the Sunday newspaper.

'Daisy! Just listen to this. "Another nasty murder in Pimlico. Woman found with all four limbs dismembered . . ."'

'Ooh, don't Mrs. Bridges!' Daisy pleaded. 'It's bad enough all on my own over the mews. Every creak sounding like a footstep . . .'

'Yes,' Mrs. Bridges said, not listening: 'and it says here the maniac murderer is on the rampage, seeking his next victim, "like a wild animal that has tasted blood and will not be denied".'

'Oh, please! Oh, why does Eddie have to be away so long?'

'He has his duty to do, same as all of us,' Mrs. Bridges answered matter-of-factly; but even she gave a start and glanced round alarmedly when they heard a noise outside the servants' hall door. The door opened and no one more sinister came through it than Mr. Hudson in his street clothes, followed by Lily in hers. Each carried a prayer book. They were very wet.

'We had a sermon about Noah and the Ark,' Lily couldn't wait to say. 'Mr. Hudson said it was very appropriate.'

'Never mind jokes, Lily,' Mrs. Bridges said. 'Mr. Hudson, his lordship's back suddenly from Scotland, by himself. He wants to see you.'

Hudson bustled out of his wet things and put on his black jacket.

'Yes,' Daisy said to Lily, 'and there's his room to be aired and dinner laid, so you get changed quick.'

The girl and Mr. Hudson left the room. Daisy started to move about her own duties, but paused to ask, wide-eyed: 'Mrs. Bridges – did they find the *head*?'

'Oh, yes. See here . . . "The severed head was found . . ." '

In Richard's study, Mr. Hudson lost no time in establishing the reason for his lordship's unexpected return.

'I trust you and her ladyship are enjoying your stay in Scotland, m'lord?'

'Very much, thank you, Hudson.'

'I, er, was distressed to read in the newspaper of the Prime Minister's illness and resignation.'

'Yes, it's a sad business. That's why I've come up to London. We have to choose a successor. Not too easy.'

'I'm sure, m'lord.'

'Hudson, who would you choose – in confidence? Mr. Baldwin or Lord Curzon?'

The butler pursed his lips judicially, but it was a matter to which he had already given thought and resolved unhesitatingly.

'Lord Curzon would be my choice.'

'Oh? Why?'

'Well, m'lord, Lord Curzon is more . . . is very much of a gentleman . . .'

Richard gave him a quizzical look, but forebore to pursue the topic.

'I believe the Major's out of town just now,' he said instead.

'That is so, m'lord. He's down in Kent for a few days' golfing.'

'Oh yes, he did say something . . . And by the way, Hudson, I'm expecting Lord Newbury round to see me any time now. He telephoned.'

'Very good, m'lord.'

The front door bell sounded.

'Ah, that will be his lordship now, no doubt. Shall I fetch some sherry?'

'Yes please, Hudson.'

The butler went out momentarily and returned briefly to usher Lord Newbury in.

Bunny was, like James, in early middle age now; but he was one of those beings, lucky in some respects if not in others, who seem ageless, stuck in some limbo of their mid-thirties. His hair remained dark and full, his face schoolboyish, his expensive brown Harris Tweed suit baggy and outsized, as if it had been a hand-down from some older brother. In fact, he had been Marquis of Newbury for many years, and, like James again, had soldiered throughout the whole, and the worst, of the war.

'Hullo, Bunny,' Richard greeted him, shaking his hand. 'How very nice to see you.'

Bunny gave him his shy smile, blinked a few times, and asked, 'Er, how are you?'

'We're all fine. How's your lovely Diana?'

'Well, quite honestly, I . . . I haven't the least idea. That's why I've come to see you.'

'Do sit down.'

'Thanks. I've been away, fishing on the Usk. No water, so I came up last night, meaning to pick Diana up at the Ritz and take her back to Somerby. But . . . she's not there. This, er, note was waiting for me at the club.'

He got out the paper from his inside pocket and handed it to Richard, whose expression changed as he read it from curiosity to horror.

'Good Lord! I honestly don't believe it.'

'Well, neither did ... I mean ... Well, where *is* James?'

Richard thought quickly and replied, 'I'm not at all sure. I'm only just back from Scotland myself, and the servants don't seem too sure ...'

Mr. Hudson had entered with the sherry tray just in time to hear this. He felt Lord Newbury's gaze on him and held his enigmatic expression.

'Extraordinary!' Lord Newbury was saying, to which Lord Bellamy responded, 'Look, Bunny, I'll find out what I can and let you know right away.'

Lord Newbury declined the drink and took his leave, saying, 'Thank you. I'll see myself out. I've a taxi waiting.'

'Don't, er ... don't do anything rash ... you know,' were Lord Bellamy's parting words.

The younger man shrugged. 'What can I do – on a Sunday?'

He went. Mr. Hudson concentrated on placing the tray symmetrically in the centre of a low table.

'Hudson,' he heard. 'Do you know the Major's telephone number in Kent?'

'Yes, m'lord. It's Deal two ...'

'Just get it for me, please. At once.'

'Very good, m'lord.'

Mr. Hudson knew better than to pause to offer sherry. There was something in his lordship's tone that made him think better, also, of listening in on the main receiver after the call had been successfully put through.

'James,' Richard said without ado. 'Is Diana Newbury down there with you?'

'Father! What an extraordinary question.'

'Look, James. I've just had Bunny here with a note he's had from Diana, saying she's run off with you.'

Diana, at James's elbow, was hissing, 'Who the hell's that?' 'My father,' he said out of the corner of his mouth. 'Yes,' he said into the mouthpiece. 'She's here.'

'For heaven's sake, James!' Richard raved. 'Have you gone quite mad?'

'Why on earth did you tell him?' Diana whispered angrily. James ignored her, listening to his father.

'I'm deadly serious, James. Come back to London straight away.'

'Yes. All right, Father. Goodbye.'

James hung up and turned away, his mouth twitching.

'*Why?*' she demanded. He rounded on her.

'Bunny's been round brandishing a note from you, saying you've run off with me. How dare you?'

She stood her ground. 'It's no use shilly-shallying. I mean, once you said I could come down here with you, I made up my mind, and I knew you'd agree.'

'Oh, did you!'

'Yes. Anyway, I didn't expect Bunny back till Wednesday. Listen, darling, let's just go as we planned. Let's leave now. It's all perfectly simple . . .'

'No. We can't go now. It'd be running away. We must go back and clear it up.'

'No!'

'*Yes!*'

'The whole thing sounds to me like an absolute farce,' an angry Richard said that evening.

'Yes, Father,' James agreed, calmly enough. 'It certainly contained some farcical elements.'

'But the consequences aren't likely to be funny. I must say, I do find your behaviour quite extraordinary. I know that morals are pretty loose these days, and having a mistress is quite the usual thing . . .'

'Diana Newbury isn't my mistress . . .'

'You know perfectly well what I mean. Good heavens, aren't there enough stray women about without your having to pick on the wife of one of your best friends – a man in your own regiment, and, what's worse than anything, a peer of the realm?'

James smiled grimly. 'If anyone did the picking, it was Diana.'

'That's a very gallant remark, I must say. It will sound

very well in court and in the gutter Press. For God's sake, can't you think of the family? I do have a certain position, you know.'

Never having cared to be put on the defensive, James counter-attacked with his usual weapon, sarcasm.

'I doubt if anything even your wicked, evil son can do would shake the rock-like foundations of your shining reputation.'

The telephone rang at his elbow. He answered it, then covered the mouthpiece, turning to his father with a surprised look.

'It's Bunny!'

Richard moved urgently. 'For heaven's sake, don't speak to him.'

It was too late; James had taken his own decision.

'Yes. Hullo, Bunny. Yes, I see. Fair enough. Well, we can't very well meet at the club. Why don't you come here? Right? Good. Goodbye.'

He hung up and rang the bell, his father watching aghast.

'You must be quite mad,' Richard said. 'Don't you understand, you must not talk with Bunny Newbury until you've seen your lawyer?'

'Why not? As you said, he is, or was, an old friend. I don't see why we can't talk this whole thing over in a civilised manner.'

'Use your brains, boy. If he wants to ruin you over this...'

'Father!' James snapped, moving on to the offensive proper. 'Thank you for all your advice, even if I didn't ask for it. I hate to say this, but while I'm delighted that you and Virginia and the children should live here, this does happen to be my house, and who I ask to come here is my business and no one else's . . . And, just this one evening, I'd be very glad if you would leave me alone.'

Pale with anger and hurt, Richard turned on his heel and strode from the room, oblivious of the presence of Hudson, who had entered in time to hear the last words.

The butler's face registered shock and disapproval. James either did not notice, or ignored it.

'Hudson, his lordship will be out to dinner, and I would like some sandwiches in here right away.'

'Yes, sir.'

'And plenty of them. I'm very hungry.'

'*Sandwiches!*' Mrs. Bridges echoed as she hurried to prepare them. 'Like it was a railway train! I don't know ... First voices raised, and his lordship slamming out of the house, and now sandwiches!'

She turned on Edward.

'What is it, Edward? That's what I'd like to know.'

He swallowed, but succeeded in standing on his dignity.

'I'm sorry, Mrs. B. I'm not in a position to divulge ...'

' "Divulge"! "Di-vulge"! Wherever did you learn such words? You are in a position to, but you won't, and that's the plain truth. We all know you was down at that cottage in Kent ...'

'Well, if you all know, why ask?'

She flourished the bread-knife at him. 'Don't you be cheeky, Edward. What I always say is that secrets don't do nobody any good. They fester inside, and cause trouble. I shall have to talk to Mr. Hudson about you, I really will. After all these years ...'

'Sorry, Mrs. Bridges,' he said humbly, glad to escape from her kitchen. In the servants' hall his wife caught up with him.

'What is happening, then?' Daisy asked.

He looked round. 'Come over here, Dais. You won't believe me, but ...'

As he whispered in her ear her eyes grew bigger and rounder.

'Oooh, Eddie!'

'Yeah. In the same bed – and not a very big one, at that. I mean, I had to take their breakfast up to them. It was ... embarrassing.'

'Well, I never did! It's like a ... a ... What's going to happen next?'

'They'll get married. I mean, they'll have to, won't they?'

'And then they'll come and live here and kick the others out.'

'No. They won't live here, because of the disgrace, you see. Violet – I mean, Lady Newbury's maid – said she heard they was talking of going to the Continent.'

'P'raps they'll take us, Eddy? Oh, no. She's got a maid.'

'Yeh.'

'What's she like?'

'Lady Newbury?'

'No, the maid.'

'Oh, Miss Marshall. She's . . .'

'You called her Violet.'

'Oh, yeh. Well, I mean, as there was only the two of us . . .'

Daisy regarded him, smiling but watchful.

'Just Violet and Eddie, eh? All alone in a tiny cottage.'

He blushed violently, annoyed to have to defend an innocence that was genuine.

'Look, there was nothing went on between us. Honest! Anyway, she's an ugly old cow, with buck teeth like a rabbit.'

He put his arms round her.

'Here, Dais . . . I missed you ever so much. I really did.'

'Beg pardon, I'm sure,' said Lily, sweeping past close to them. 'Lord Newbury's back upstairs.'

'What, again?' Daisy exclaimed.

'That's what Mr. Hudson said.'

It was indeed the Marquis of Newbury whom Mr. Hudson had shown into the Major's presence in the study, a few seconds after delivering a generous plateful of sandwiches there. He paused briefly outside the door, listening, but heard only the low murmur of voices, and went back downstairs.

Anything less like the avenging lion than Bunny Newbury could not have been imagined.

'I know this isn't the way I should be behaving,' he told James apologetically, fidgeting with his feet and not knowing what to do with his hands. 'I ought to be threatening to knock you down, and beating Diana, and sending all over the place for lawyers . . . That sort of thing.'

James, seated in his armchair, seemed very much in command of the situation. He gestured towards the settee.

'I'm very glad you've come,' he said. 'Have a sandwich.'

Happy to have found some positive activity, Bunny took one, thanked him, and sat down. He took a small bite, then said, 'I've thought an awful lot about this, James, and I realise that it isn't entirely your fault . . . or Diana's, come to that. You knew her before I did and I've always known how fond she was of you. I probably shouldn't have married her in the first place, but Mother was very keen. In those days I was very inexperienced in the ways of the world.'

'You were, rather, I remember,' James smiled.

'I was desperately shy, that was one of my troubles. I haven't been a very good husband, I suppose.'

'A lot better than most.'

'Well . . . nice of you to say so. I admit I've rather taken Diana for granted.'

'Do you . . . do you love her still?'

'It's such a . . . funny word. Yes, I think I do. There's never been anyone else. I'm going to miss her most awfully. But what I really came here to say, James, was that I'm not going to divorce Diana under any circumstances. If you tell me that she truly loves you, and that you love her and will . . . you know, look after her and all that, then I'll give her grounds to divorce me.'

'That's very decent of you, Bunny,' James said steadily.

'Well, I was brought up to believe that no man should divorce a woman. It may sound a bit old-fashioned, but I think it's right.'

'Yes.'

Bunny got up, putting his unfinished sandwich down in an ashtray.

'So, I'd be very grateful if you could talk to Diana about it, James. I don't think I could face her, just at present.'

James got up, too.

'Yes, yes. I'll have to do a bit of thinking and then I will. I'll let you know. Goodbye, Bunny.'

'Goodbye, James.'

And they parted company as though they had been bidding one another goodnight on the club doorstep.

'I wish he wasn't being so nice about it,' Diana complained to James next day. 'It makes it all so difficult. Perhaps it was being nice made him such a dud as a lover, and me such a dud at being loved.'

'You're not a dud at being loved,' James protested. He paused, then added, 'It seems I should ask you to marry me.'

'How d'you mean "it seems"?'

'Well, isn't that the next move in the game?'

'Why don't you make it, then?'

'Diana, darling, before I do, I think we must be very honest with each other . . .'

She gave a little puff of exasperation. 'Must we? That sounds terribly boring. And it hurts so – being honest.'

'Bunny wants me to promise him that if I marry you I will make you happy.'

'How can anyone promise that? Anyway, you do.'

'No. I don't even think I do. I don't think I can.'

'Why?'

'I mean, even in those few days we had rows.'

'That was just because we were so cooped up.'

'If you're married, you have to survive being cooped up.'

Diana sighed heavily and let her shoulders sag. For once, the light of excitement and quick thought went from her eyes.

'Oh, dear. It's all my fault. I always think I'm right. James, darling, I wasn't all selfish when I saw you in that dive with that woman – yes, I spotted her. You were all alone, really, and you looked so . . . so lost and lonely. I just wanted to wrap a warm mantle of . . . of feeling wanted round you. To make you feel that someone loved you and needed you. I thought there was still a spark and that I could blow it back into flame.'

James could feel his temporary good spirits draining away. The familiar old leaden weight was beginning to settle itself on him once more. He said morosely, 'The spark was snuffed out five years ago, in the mud of Passchendaele Ridge. I'm a fraud, Diana. I'm not the James Bellamy you once fell in love with. I'm counterfeit.'

'That's nonsense. You can't blame everything on the war. You've got to pull yourself together and get on with life again.'

He was already too far gone for a pep talk to help him.

'I've tried, honestly I have. It hasn't worked. I mean, I'm not particularly unhappy. Things just don't seem worth doing. I'm quite content just sitting comfortably, watching the world go by ... success ... love ... Yes, I'll marry you, Diana, but you must know the terms.'

'I don't want you to marry me out of decency. James, what are we to do?'

He shook his head slowly as her eyes searched his glum face in vain.

'I don't know,' he said. 'I haven't got as far as that yet.'

Two mornings later he had still not thought it out. Once more he had retired to the seclusion of his own room, and so did not see the large motor car which stopped outside the house, nor see the woman who got out of it and went down the area steps. He would have recognised her; but Daisy didn't when she opened the door to her.

'I wish to see Mr. Barnes,' the woman said, in a superior tone.

'I'm sorry,' Daisy said, polite but curious; 'Mr. Barnes is not available. I'm Mrs. Barnes, if I can help you.'

'Oh,' said the visitor, 'so you're Daisy. Well, I am Miss Marshall, Lady Newbury's maid.'

'Pleased to meet you, I'm sure.'

'I've got a note from Lady Newbury to Major Bellamy. I wanted Edward to deliver it personally.'

'If you'll leave it with me, Miss Marshall, I will see that it's delivered personally.'

'That's frightfully good of you, Daisy,' Violet said, handing over the envelope. 'Now I must rush. I've got to pick up Lady Newbury. Lord Newbury's taking us on a cruise, so there's so much to organise.'

'Oh!'

'Give Edward my kind regards, and tell him from me that I think he's very lucky to have such a pretty little wife.'

Restraining herself, Daisy replied, 'I'm sure my husband will be desolated that he missed you, Miss Marshall.'

Violet took a grand departure, leaving Daisy seething. As soon as Edward came in, minutes later, she sniffed ostentatiously and wafted the air with her hand.

'What's all that for?' Edward asked.

'Can't you smell the sweet perfume that fills the air?'

'Eh? Come on, Dais.'

'An old friend of yours called while you were out.'

'Who?'

' "An ugly old cow with buck teeth" according to you.'

'Not Vi . . . Miss Marshall?'

'She sent her kind regards, but couldn't wait as she was going on a cruise. Don't you wish you was going, too?'

'Don't be daft, Dais. But are *they* going – the Newburys?'

'Seems like it.'

'Then it's all come out right. I'm glad.'

'There's a note from *her* to the Major. You're to deliver it personal.'

He did. James read it when he was alone and then took it with him, in search of his father. He found him in the study.

'I gather Bunny's talked to you again – or rather, you've talked to him.'

'He wanted my advice.'

'He seems to have taken it. Thanks, Father.'

Richard smiled at last. 'Well, I've had quite a lot of experience, one way and another. You know, James, I seem to have been getting you out of scrapes since you first went to school.'

'Yes. I'm sorry. And I'm sorry I was rude to you the other evening. It was inexcusable. I wasn't quite myself, I'm afraid.'

Richard went to him and put his arm round him.

'Look – now Baldwin's settled in I'm lunching at No. 10, then going back to Scotland tonight. Why don't you come with me?'

James shook his head. 'Thanks all the same. I'll be all right.'

His father hesitated, then said, 'For all our sakes, James – do try and be more sensible.'

James nodded and went away to his room. The sound of his gramophone was shortly heard throughout the house. Downstairs, the concensus of opinion was that the Major was 'himself' again.

CHAPTER SIX

GEORGINA, back from America, was enthusing to Richard and Virginia about the experience.

'And when we docked this morning there were thousands of people on the quay, cheering and screaming for Douglas Fairbanks and Mary Pickford. I thought we'd never get down the gangway.'

'Did you see them close-to?' Virginia asked, quite agog.

'Oh, yes. They walked round the Promenade Deck every morning, however rough it was.'

'Well,' Richard smiled, 'you seem to have enjoyed the voyage. How was New York?'

'Oh, so thrilling. I wish you could see Elizabeth's apartment. It's on the 14th floor, overlooking the Hudson River. Hudson! That's appropriate, isn't it? You know, she's longing for James to go over and stay with them. I've got all sorts of messages for him. He is a bore, going off to France like that when he knew I was due.'

Richard said wistfully, 'He wanted to tour the battle-fields and visit the graves of some of his friends. I sometimes feel the poor chap has more affinity with them than with the living.'

'Well . . . Anyway, Virginia, how are the children?'

'They're at the sea for Easter. William's loving Summer Fields. He got quite a good report. Alice is at day school now – Miss Faunce's.'

Mr. Hudson entered and announced luncheon.

'You must be ravenous after all that sea air,' Richard said to his niece as he took her in. 'I expect Virginia told you we're due at the opening of the Wembley Exhibition this afternoon. Sorry to desert you so soon, but it's an official invitation just for the two of us.'

'Oh, I'll go some other time,' Georgina replied. 'It'll take me the whole afternoon unpacking.'

'Ruby,' Daisy said one afternoon. 'You seen Lily?'

'Not since lunch.'

Daisy scowled. 'She's supposed to be upstairs, helping me. I've whistled for her twice and nobody answered, so I've had to come all the way down.'

'I heard Mr. Hudson telling her she could go round to the shops sometime to buy her mother's birthday present.'

'Oh, he did, did he? Well, that does it!'

She stamped through to the butler's pantry and entered uninvited. Mr. Hudson took off his round steel spectacles and frowned up at her from his seat at his table.

'Knock when you come into the pantry, Daisy,' he reminded her.

'I forgot.' He could not mistake the defiance in her tone. 'I want to know where Lily is.'

'She is out, posting a letter for me.'

'That's not what Ruby says.'

'Never mind what Ruby says.'

'Now, look here, Mr. Hudson, Lily's supposed to be my under-housemaid. There's work to be done upstairs and she's never here when I want her these days.'

'I am in charge of the staff, Daisy, not you.'

'I know you are. But that doesn't explain why Ruby tells me one thing and you say something else. Lily's been allowed to go out shopping and everything's left to me. Does she get special favours or something in this house?'

'Hold your tongue, girl,' Hudson snapped. 'And get out of my pantry.'

'With pleasure. I just hope the work gets done proper, that's all, because I'm not doing it on my own.'

She shut the door behind her with unnecessary firmness and marched past Ruby into the kitchen, where Mrs. Bridges was working at the table.

'Blinking butler's pet!' Daisy stormed.

'What's all that?' Mrs. Bridges demanded.

'I'm looking for Lily. She's not here to help me, because Mr. Hudson's let her go out. Does what she likes these days, if you ask me. Or what *he* likes.'

' "*He!*" Daisy, how dare you say such things? You're not to speak like that.'

'Butler's pet!' Daisy repeated, as Rose came through from the servants' hall.

'What's all the squabbling?' she asked.

'Nothing.'

'Didn't sound like nothing. Where's Lily?'

'Don't ask me.'

'I just did. I've got some mending for her.'

'Well, I've got some work for her. As for where she is, try asking *him*.'

She jerked her head pantry-wards, glared at Mrs. Bridges, and stalked away.

That evening Georgina went into Virginia's boudoir, to find Rose assisting her with her evening dress.

'Just in time, darling,' Virginia smiled. 'You can tell me whether to wear my pearls or these beads. We're dining with the Fitzaland-Howards and there's going to be a bishop there.'

'Should you wear jewellery at all for a bishop?'

'I'm not sure. It's a Roman Catholic bishop.'

'Then wear the beads – like a Rosary.'

Rose joined in their giggles.

'Your bag and gloves are on the bed, m'lady,' she said.

'Thank you, Rose. There isn't anything else.'

Rose left. Virginia adjusted the beads and said to herself in the mirror, 'I suppose beads aren't quite as voluptuous as pearls.' She addressed Georgina's reflection. 'What did you think of Wembley?'

'Oh, marvellous. Only, Virginia . . . I'm not sure whether I ought to mention something to you, but it seemed a bit odd . . .'

Virginia turned. 'What did?'

'Well, in one of the African pavilions, where some Gold Coast natives were weaving mats, I suddenly saw Hudson – just a glimpse of him through the crowd.'

'It was his afternoon off. Everyone's going to Wembley.'

'You may well say that. He had Lily with him.'

'Lily? Our Lily?'

'Yes. They didn't see me, of course.'

'Well, I suppose he wanted to show her the exhibition. You know what he's like – rather schoolmasterly, I've always thought.'

'Are schoolmasters supposed to hold their pupils' hands?'

'Georgina! You don't mean to say . . . !'

'Absolutely certain. You don't blame me for mentioning it?'

'I think it's probably as well you did. I thought Lily was such a quiet, respectable girl. As to Hudson . . . ! I suppose there must be some innocent explanation, but I'll really have to make some tactful enquiries.'

She naturally turned to Rose when next they found themselves alone.

'Rose, you're the one who knows most about the others downstairs. I've noticed lately that Lily seems a little . . . quiet, subdued. Is she all right?'

'Far as I know, m'lady.'

'You don't get the impression that she's unsettled, or worried about anything?'

'Not to my knowledge.'

'Do you happen, by any chance, to know if she has a young man? Someone she meets on her days off?'

'I couldn't say, m'lady,' Rose said, her face expressionless. But she knew very well what her ladyship was hinting, and as soon as she could get Lily alone she intended to drag it into the open.

Her chance came quickly; the next evening, in fact. Lily had been taking her twice-weekly bath and was sitting on her bed in her cheap, flowered dressing gown, combing her hair. Rose knocked and entered.

'Hullo, Lily,' she smiled. 'Nice bath?'

'Yes, thanks.'

'Water still warm enough?'

'Oh, yes.'

'That's good.' Rose paused, then went on: 'I wanted a word, private like.'

'What about?'

'I thought you ought to know her ladyship asked me this morning if I thought you had a young man.'

'What did you say?'

'I didn't know.'

Lily nodded dumbly, volunteering nothing more.

Rose added, 'There is someone, though – isn't there?'

'I . . . I'd rather not say, Rose.'

'Look, I know there's someone. Everybody downstairs does.'

Lily looked startled. 'They don't!'

Rose nodded. 'Most of us have been living amongst each other too long not to notice when there's . . . there's any change. Lily, it's best to be truthful, and I promise I won't tell. It's . . . Mr. Hudson – isn't it?'

Lily looked down miserably, and barely audibly said, 'If her ladyship knew I'd get notice, wouldn't I?'

'He would, more likely.'

'Oh, not Mr. Hudson!'

'It is him, then?'

Lily could only nod again. Then she said animatedly, 'He's done nothing wrong, Rose. He's been ever so good and kind to me, telling me all sorts of interesting things about foreign parts and all that, and he takes me to museums. One night he took me to a real music concert at the Albert Hall. It was beautiful music, Rose. Only, it's just that . . .'

'What, Lily?'

'Oh, nothing.'

'What happens after these concerts and museums and things?'

'We have some tea sometimes – in a teashop.'

'And then?'

'We talk for a bit. Or rather, he does – all serious about people needing happiness and . . . love . . . and things. He's a very clever man, Rose. He can't half use words. But after a while he stops himself and we come home. He waits about round the corner while I go in first, so's not to come in together.'

Rose pursed her lips. 'I bet he does.'

'Please, Rose – you won't tell anyone.'

'I've promised not to, haven't I?'

But, as she had told the unhappy girl, others had been putting two and two together. Nothing had been discussed, though, and in fact the unavoidable crisis was precipitated by silence – Rose's silence that same evening when Mr. Hudson asked her if her ladyship was in her room upstairs.

'I asked you a question, Rose,' he said sharply. She still didn't answer, and walked pointedly up the stairs and out through the pass door, never moving her head when he called her name.

He turned to Mrs. Bridges, with whom he was left alone. 'That was insubordinate and quite uncalled for!' he fumed. 'I shall take the girl to task in front of her ladyship, if necessary.'

Mrs. Bridges raised a sorrowful eyebrow.

'I can only suppose she feels strongly about . . . well, you know what, Mr. Hudson.'

'I don't know . . .'

'Oh yes, you do, Angus. We all do.'

He opened his mouth to retort, but no words came. He stared at her for some moments, then lowered his gaze and said, 'What am I to do, Kate?'

'You must do what you feel is right, Angus. I can't advise you. It's not for me to tell you how to live your life.'

'I can hardly expect you to understand,' he muttered. 'You of all people.'

'If you've decided you're . . . in love with her, or something, well, that's nobody's business except yours and hers. She's a nice enough girl – modest and clean and decent. But have you thought about your position here? I mean, it's not exactly usual. Butlers in good houses don't go out with young housemaids. It's going against all you've stood for over the years, Angus. All what's proper and respectable.'

Mr. Hudson bridled. 'There is nothing that is not respectable in my situation, Mrs. Bridges. And nothing unusual, other than Lily's extreme youth.'

'That's what I mean. If it was some woman more your own age . . .'

He was stammering, 'I . . . I believe it is her youth that inspires me, more than anything else. She makes me feel that my . . . my future is . . . worthwhile.'

Mrs. Bridges made no answer. Thoughts and memories chased one another in her mind, and unhappiness welled. The silence between them was a long one. Then, at last, he said, 'I'm going up now to see if her ladyship is alone. If so, I must consult her.'

'Yes, Angus,' she said, her voice more than usually husky. 'I think you should.'

She watched him go sorrowfully.

Virginia was by herself in the morning room, writing a letter at the desk. As soon as she saw the expression on Hudson's face she knew what it was that he was requesting to discuss with her. She got up and stood facing him. He swallowed and commenced.

'I feel it my duty, m'lady, in all honesty, to inform you that I have become extremely attached in a personal way to . . . to Lily, the under-housemaid.'

Virginia regarded him steadily, showing neither surprise nor curiosity. He was obliged to plough on.

'I have to confess that over recent weeks I have developed very deep feelings towards the girl, young though she may be. I have been attempting to instruct her in many things. To open her eyes to the world outside. To teach her to better herself, and so forth, with a view to eventual marriage.'

Virginia had to react now.

'Are you telling me that you wish to marry Lily?'

'I have come to respect, love and cherish the young person, m'lady. I trust your ladyship will not doubt my sincerity.'

'But Hudson, Lily is only just twenty-two.'

He ignored the point. 'We have been sharing our time off for some little while, visiting museums together, picture galleries, places of historic interest . . . delighting in each other's company.'

'But are you quite sure that Lily's feelings aren't simply those of a young girl who's flattered by the attentions of an older man? It's possible that she sees you more as a father or a kindly uncle than as . . . as a man she might wish to marry!'

'She has brought a new meaning to my life, m'lady.'

'Yes, but has she actually told you she is in love with you?'

'She has indicated her gratitude for my attentions, m'lady. She has allowed me to . . . express my . . . my affection for her . . . without, of course, in any way . . .'

He tailed off unhappily. At that moment the door opened and Richard came in. Virginia lost no time in apprising him of the situation. His mind reeled.

'What . . . what do you propose to do, Hudson?' he asked weakly.

'In the circumstances, m'lord, it would of course be quite unsuitable for me to continue as butler here. So I must ask you to accept one month's notice, if that will be convenient.'

'It's hardly convenient at all, Hudson,' Richard snapped, and turned away to where the whisky waited. Virginia nodded an indication that the interview was at an end and the butler withdrew.

'It's beyond belief!' Richard raged as soon as the door closed. 'That a man of his character should be willing to abdicate – that's the only word for it – to abdicate entirely his authority and position in this house; to throw up all he's achieved and built up over the years for the sake of some ignorant chit of a girl, less than half his age . . .'

He swallowed whisky recklessly. Virginia said, 'It's not entirely unknown, Richard. Perhaps he's reaching out, as men sometimes do at his time of life, to grasp at something he's always dreamed of but never achieved.'

'Huh! What?'

'Some sort of ideal vision of love and marriage, before it's too late.'

Richard snorted again, tossed off the contents of his glass, refilled it, then voiced what was concerning him most.

'We'll never find another butler like Hudson.'

Virginia smiled, causing him to scowl even more. She took his arm.

'Darling, no one's indispensable. You're the one who's always said that. Frederick can perfectly well announce dinner and clean the silver and open the door to visitors. It's not the end of the world.'

But he would not be mollified. 'It would never be the same, Virginia. Never. Damn the man!'

Below stairs, the object of his disgruntlement sat brooding at the table in his pantry. He lifted his head at a tap on the door and heard Lily asking if she might come in.

'You said it was all right to come to the pantry and talk to you if I was ever worried,' she explained when he had closed the door behind her. She went to stand at the other side of the table from him.

'That's quite all right, Lily. What is it?'

'They all know about us. Don't they? Everyone in this house.'

He had to nod.

'What are they saying, Mr. Hudson? What do they think of us?'

'What they say or think should not concern you, my dear. The important thing is that our feelings for one another are now generally known. Our friendship is out in the open at last. There will be no further need for our small untruths and deceptions.'

'I see,' she faltered. 'That's . . . all right, then.'

He could tell that she was seeking words to say something more, but discretion led him to go to the door.

'You must return to your room before anyone hears you,'

he told her. 'Try not to be anxious. We have nothing shameful to hide.'

'No, Mr. Hudson,' she said in a tone devoid of conviction. 'I'm sorry I disturbed you.'

'Run along, then, my dear,' he smiled and ushered her out without touching her.

Frederick said to her next morning, 'He must be proper gone on you to give in his notice. I mean, he's got a good job here.'

'I know he has,' Lily answered unhappily. Her gloom was apparent to all except Mr. Hudson, who bore the air of a man under hypnosis.

She went on, 'I've told him I'm not sure about marrying or anything like that. It frightens me. If only he could . . . well, find someone else to love. Some nice woman. I mean, I like him. He's always been nice to me. So I just can't bring myself to . . . to tell him I don't fancy him. I couldn't stand to hurt him that much.'

'You can't go on dangling him on a string.'

'I don't know what to do, Fred. He wants to go to my home at Banbury and see my mother. I don't want him going there, but he wants to go on Sunday and take me with him.'

'You'll have to say something to him soon, then, else you'll wake up one day and find yourself at the altar.'

That was a growing fear which Lily took to bed with her at nights and found awaiting her again each morning.

'Get me out a plain scarf, will you, Rose?' Virginia requested later that morning. They were in Virginia's boudoir. She was dressing to go to a meeting of the committee of the Naval Education Fund, the body in whose cause she had first come to this house during the war and had so irritated the man who was to come to love and marry her.

That same man came in now, clearly irritated once again.

'Hudson's just been up to see me,' he growled. 'No, don't go, Rose. You might as well hear this too. He's going to see Lily's mother at Banbury.'

'Whatever for?' Virginia asked, wide-eyed.

'To ask for her consent to the marriage.'

Rose's mouth fell open.

'He means it,' Richard said. 'He says he's given the matter careful thought and he intends, with our permission, to go there with Lily on Sunday. I just thought you'd like to know.'

He stalked out again.

Rose told Virginia, 'I would like to say, m'lady, that I'm very sorry this has happened. You and his lordship have my deepest sympathy.'

'You mustn't worry on our behalf, Rose. We'll survive. Ask Edward to have the car ready for eleven o'clock, please. Oh, and better ask Mrs. Bridges to step up about the meals.'

That good lady made her way upstairs with her pencil and pad. Virginia, however, could see that she was upset and in no state to discuss culinary matters.

'We're all upset downstairs, my lady,' Mrs. Bridges answered her solicitous inquiry.

Her lower lip trembled.

'I just can't understand it. You see, years ago, m'lady, when I was in a bit of trouble with the police, Hudson helped me and stood by me. He spoke up for me in court, and, like, gave me to understand that if ever he thought of getting married one day it'd be me he'd ask to be his partner in life. And I told him I would always be . . . like, holding myself in reservation for him. But now . . . but now . . . I don't know what's come over him, m'lady. I really don't.'

'I know how worrying it must be for you especially, Mrs. Bridges,' said Virginia, who knew all about the one indiscretion in her cook's past. 'Perhaps we'd better postpone doing the meals until I get back. Come up at tea-time, will you?'

As she watched Mrs. Bridges go, her thought was 'Hudson! Hudson! What are you doing to us all?'

Georgina asked that question out loud that evening. At least, she did so metaphorically, and it was Lily whom she addressed as the girl was closing the morning-room curtains.

'You do know, don't you, Lily, that Hudson's leaving us because of you?'

Lily turned to face her, but found it hard to meet the gaze of those beautiful eyes.

'Yes, I do, miss.'

'And you'll be leaving as well, I imagine, so that you can both get married.'

'Well, Miss Georgina, I . . . I don't know. It's all muddled.'

'Does Hudson think you're willing to marry him?'

'I think he does, Miss.'

'And you? Or don't you want to talk about it? You don't have to.'

'Oh, no, miss, I don't mind talking about it to you.'

'Then what's the matter, Lily? Are you worried about Hudson's age? Or is it that you're frightened to tell him how you really feel?'

Lily burst out urgently, 'Miss, I've got to speak to him. Before tomorrow, 'cos he's taking me on the train to Banbury to see my mother, and I don't know what to do.'

'Tell me everything, Lily,' Georgina said gently. 'Perhaps I can help in some way, if you'd like me to.'

The girl poured out her feelings, growing in articulation as her mind unburdened. Georgina prompted her with questions. She was no intellectual, but she was a beautiful young woman who had seen a good deal of life, and in these circumstances that was more important.

And next morning, when Mr. Hudson, wearing his best suit with a yellow rose in his buttonhole and carrying a bunch of tulips and a small cake in a presentation box, came looking for Lily, she bit her lip and said, 'I'm sorry, Mr. Hudson, but I'm not going with you to see my mother. There's no point.'

'But there's every point, my dear,' he said. 'I would never dream of embarking on marriage without at least visiting the parent of . . .'

'I'm not going to marry you, Mr. Hudson. You haven't asked me to, anyway.'

'Lily, it has been understood ever since . . .'

'I never, never said I'd marry you.'

'You have never denied your feelings for me. Have I not been entitled to assume your consent?'

'No, you haven't. I don't wish to marry you, Mr. Hudson, because you're not a romantic person for a young girl.'

'But you've said over and over again how much you've enjoyed learning, accompanying me to interesting places . . . You're tired and strained, child. Try . . .'

'I'm not tired or strained, thank you. I just don't love you. When I marry I want to marry a young man who's strong and good-looking and romantic. Someone who can take me in his arms and make love to me and give me babies.'

'Lily . . . !'

'Yes, and laugh with me and make jokes. I don't want to spend my whole life in and out of museums and getting lectured about art and all that. Do you call that loving someone?'

Hudson found himself pleading.

'I have given in my notice here, Lily. I have thrown away my whole career as a gesture of my love for you. Why have you not spoken like this before?'

'Because I've always been afraid of you . . . What you'd say. I went out with you when you asked me because it was something to do on my days off. But I don't fancy you. I want a young man to marry me, not some old schoolteacher who talks Scotch and all about history and God and things and never touches me but holds my hand on a park bench or on top of a bus when it's dark and no one can see. That's not love. No, I wouldn't marry you, Mr. Hudson, not if there was nobody else left in the world. No, please go away and leave me alone.'

Hudson, pale-faced from the harsh and breathless attack, managed to say, through half-frozen lips, 'It seems . . . I have made quite a wee fool of myself. I must apologise to you, Lily. I ought to have known better. I'll go and change out of these things.'

He went away. Lily realised that she was trembling. She marvelled that she had found the courage to speak out in the way that Miss Georgina had urged she should. But she was profoundly relieved that she had.

An air of tension seemed to hang over the whole house that day. As it was Sunday, the staff were in contact with one another less than on other days. Hudson remained for most of the time in his pantry; Lily stayed in her room. Their recent custom of disappearing one after the other on a Sunday afternoon for what was meant to be taken for separate walks was not followed. The other servants looked at one another and wondered, but none ventured to question either of them.

The following morning Hudson stood once more before Lord and Lady Bellamy in the morning-room.

'What is it, Hudson?' Richard asked without attempting to soften his tone or offer the understanding of a smile.

'I merely wished to say, m'lord, that Lily has evidently left the house.'

'Left?' Virginia echoed.

'Early this morning, m'lady, without giving notice. Ruby saw her getting dressed and then she was gone. Her cupboard is empty.'

He turned his gaze to Richard.

'It would seem, m'lord, that my affections for the girl were misplaced. I had misjudged her character. From a conversation with her yesterday, it became clear to me that hers is in reality an ungenerous, cruel and somewhat malicious nature. I . . . realise I was wrong in my estimation of her.'

'I see. Er, what do you wish to do then, Hudson?'

'In view of the circumstances, m'lord, I wonder if you would require me to continue in your service.'

'Of course we would,' Virginia intervened before Richard could reply. He had been about to say the same thing, though more reservedly.

'I very much regret the incident, m'lady,' Hudson said.

'That's quite all right, Hudson. I think the sooner it is all forgotten, the better. I can't vouch for the others downstairs, but so far as his lordship and I are concerned the matter need never be mentioned again in this house.'

'Very good, m'lady. Thank you, m'lord.'

Hudson bowed and left the room. He went straight to his pantry, ignoring the other servants' questioning looks. Then he took out the letter that had been found by Ruby in Lily's room.

As he was ripping open the envelope there came a tentative tapping on the door. He paused and called, and Mrs. Bridges came in.

'I'll not stop long,' she said. 'Just to say, well, I'm sorry ... but I'm glad.'

'Yes, Kate.'

'Is that Lily's letter?'

He nodded and drew it from the envelope. He glanced over it swiftly, then read aloud, with unaccustomed emotion in his voice.

' "Dear Mr. Hudson,

I'm sorry I said all the nasty things I said, because I didn't mean it. I only wanted you to give up caring for me and make you think I was not a nice person. I really think you are a kind man and the times we had together were very happy times I shall always remember.

I'll look for another place now. One last favour, will you be so kind as ask her ladyship to forward a reference to above address which is my home you never come to in the end.

Your affectionate
Lily".'

Mrs. Bridges said huskily, 'I'm just going up to her ladyship now. I'll ask about the reference, if you like. She's sure to give it.'

Hudson nodded, unable to speak.

Mrs. Bridges touched his shoulder before turning to go.

'I'll not be long, Angus. You stop here, and when I come back I'll make you a nice cup of tea.'

CHAPTER SEVEN

Perhaps romance is contagious in a close community. Or perhaps Fate, having contributed an absurd situation to amuse itself with, finds the act agreeable and wants to do it again before moving on to other business. In seeking an even more bizarre subject for its attentions than Mr. Hudson, Fate could not have chosen better than Ruby.

That awkward, fumbling semi-literate stood in the servants' hall one morning clutching the bundle of envelopes which an astonished Hudson had just handed to her. She was smirking in a fashion that was almost repellent in its sickliness.

'Whatever is she doing with all them letters?' Mrs. Bridges demanded of Hudson, as though Ruby were not standing within four feet of her.

'Ah, now, Mrs. Bridges,' Hudson said, 'I think that Ruby, like the rest of us, is entitled to her privacy.'

'Thank you, Mr. Hudson,' the girl simpered, and went away to deal with her correspondence.

'I know what it is!' Rose declared when Ruby reappeared with the opened letters in her hand. 'You answered that advertisement for a pen-pal.'

'No, I didn't.'

Something fluttered to the floor from her grasp. Frederick moved quicker than she did and had a good glance at it before handing it back.

'Really!' Mrs. Bridges ejaculated. 'Bringing all those letters into the house from perfect strangers. You throw them on the fire this minute. Why, you don't know where they've been.'

'I won't.'

'Ruby!'

The girl turned to Hudson.

'I don't have to, Mr. Hudson, do I?'

'Well, I really . . . You can hardly write to them all.'

'Oh, no. I'll only write to one.'

'How are you going to choose?' Rose wanted to know.

'I already have.'

'Is it the fellow in the photograph?' asked the knowing Frederick. 'Come on. Read us his letter.'

'Yeh. Go on, Ruby,' Rose urged.

Ruby blushed coyly, but unfolded one of the sheets of paper.

' "Dear Madam",' she began.

'Madam, indeed!' from Mrs. Bridges. Ruby ignored her.

' "I should very much like to engage in correspondence with you. I am thirty-five years old, a bachelor, of a quiet dispos . . . dispos . . ." '

' "Disposition," I imagine,' Hudson offered.

'Oh, go on, Ruby,' Mrs. Bridges snorted impatiently. 'Let Mr. Hudson read it out. Or Rose.'

'I will,' Rose volunteered and took the letter before Ruby could protest. She launched straight into it.

> ' "Dear Madam,
>   I should very much like to engage in correspondence with you. I am thirty-five years old, a bachelor, of a quiet disposition. I live at home with my invalid parents, and am employed as a clerk in the Post Office. I like Hugh Walpole . . ."

'Who's Hugh Walpole, Mr. Hudson?'

'A novelist, Rose. A popular novelist.'

'Oh.'

> 'I like Hugh Walpole and H. G. Wells. I am fond of good music, and listen to it on the wireless, though I do sometimes go to the Queen's Hall. I hope that, if your tastes are similar, you will send me your name and address, with a view to further correspondence and possibly acquaintanceship.
>   Yours truly,
>   Herbert Turner." '

'Similar tastes!' Mrs. Bridges declared. '*Ruby?*'

'You want to be careful,' Rose warned as she handed the letter back. 'He might be Jack the Ripper.'

Frederick asked, 'If he doesn't know your name and address, how has he written to you?'

'The newspaper sent all the letters on. I just had to fill in a form – not more than twenty words – and they printed it. I put "Genteel young lady wishes to correspond with eligible young man".'

Mrs. Bridges rolled her eyes ceiling-ward.

Ruby asked, 'I can write to him, can't I, Mr. Hudson?'

'I, er, suppose so, Ruby. It's not what I would recommend, corresponding with a stranger.'

Ruby produced the photograph Fred had picked up for her.

'He looks just like Rudolph Valentino,' she cooed wetly.

Rose took the picture from her and examined it, passing it on to the others. Not her idea of Valentino, exactly. More like a Post Office clerk. Still, she thought, the poor chap had yet to see Ruby.

In the morning-room, Richard said with an unusually diffident air, 'Virginia, I wonder if you would do something for me?'

She raised her eyebrows. 'You sound very doubtful. I'm just trying to think what you could possibly ask me to do that I wouldn't be prepared to.'

'Nothing very desperate. I wondered if you would invite Guy Paynter to lunch?'

'Why, of course. Whom would you like me to ask with him? Mrs. Merivale, I suppose, if she's still his current . . . hostess.'

'That sounds like an echo of one of Prue's cattier comments.'

'It was. She told me that Sir Guy Paynter has paid attention at different times, to three widows and two divorcees, and married none of them, so she wondered how long Polly Merivale would last.'

'Darling, Paynter, like any other rich bachelor, needs a hostess – a pretty, charming, unattached woman to preside over his dinner-table and help him with his house-parties. They understand the situation perfectly, and so does everyone else. I assure you, he's not the kind of man you need hesitate to have inside your home.'

Virginia laughed out. 'Richard, how absurd you are! Of course he shall come. I merely want to know who else. We owe Lady Bush, and the Bannisters . . .'

'I thought, er, something rather more intimate. Just ourselves, Prudence, and perhaps James.'

'I thought he always had such big, lavish parties.'

'I think I'd better tell you the truth. The fact is that Guy Paynter is very influential and he uses his influence politically. He's a friend of Baldwin's and of Beaverbrook's. He quite often goes to Max's little "cabinet meetings" at Fulham.'

'And you want him to persuade Lord Beaverbrook to give more support to the United Nations in his papers.'

'No, no. I've, er, heard . . . well, Winston told me, that the Under Secretary for Foreign Affairs is resigning on his doctor's orders.'

'And you'll be offered the post?'

'I'd like it very much, but I don't think I'll be offered it. I've been out of the Government so long that they all think of me as an Elder Statesman.'

'Nonsense!'

'Exactly. I know that we were told we'd made such a mess of things with the war, and that afterwards we must leave it to the younger men. But the young men are either dead or cynical. I feel I've still an active part to play. I've a lot of experience to put to use.'

'Of course you have,' Virginia agreed readily, but she frowned a little. 'But surely the Government are all friends of yours? Winston, Austen Chamberlain, Mr. Baldwin . . . Surely you could just . . .'

'I can't very well go and say "I know you think I'm too old, but I'm not".'

'Not in those words. But...'

'I wouldn't dream of embarrassing myself, or them. But if someone like Guy Paynter casually mentioned my name in connection with the post... Said that I'd been very active with the League and working on the Treaty... He is very influential, you know.'

No more fervent champion of Richard Bellamy's qualities than Virginia existed. She felt unease and vague distaste that he should have to resort to such tactics to gain a preferment which, in her view, he was entitled to ask for straight out. But she had seen enough evidence of his life-long unwillingness to be seen to be pushing himself.

'Money talks,' she said cynically. 'Well, of course I'll gladly invite him. But you know I'm hopeless at politics.'

Richard gave her his little crooked smile.

'My dear, just be your own charming self and you'll captivate him without even trying.'

And that was what she did; though it was not her charm that made the deepest impression on him.

They had finished the meal and were taking coffee in the morning-room. Sir Guy Paynter, middle-aged but youthful in appearance, with fair hair and a chubby, slightly florid face, had begun the evening a trifle warily, as if surprised to have been invited and wondering what could be behind it. But Polly Merivale, whom Virginia had decided to ask after all, knew his conversational foibles and drew him out skilfully. Mrs. Bridges' excellent cooking obviously came as a surprise and a pleasure to him, and by the time coffee was reached he had put all his reservations aside.

'I have always believed,' he declared as he took cream and sugar from Frederick, 'that the less politicians do, the better. That's why I moved heaven and earth to make Baldwin Prime Minister instead of Curzon.'

'I didn't realise you were responsible,' James said, disliking the brash claim.

'I played my part among others. I approve of Baldwin because he never does anything at all if he can possibly help it. Things always sort themselves out, left to their own devices. It's the violent action taken by politicians which turns an unfortunate situation into a disaster.'

Glancing at Richard, Virginia perceived that he was not too happy. Such sentiments scarcely coincided with his hopes.

Polly went on encouraging Paynter to talk.

'What do you think the ideal Member of Parliament should do, then?'

'What he always does, fortunately – spend all his time arguing about things which don't matter in the very least. Look at Parliament's present exploit – debating the abolition of the death penalty for cowardice in the field.'

Both Richard and James looked sharply at Virginia and saw that her expression had frozen. They would have been too late to head Paynter off, though.

'We fight a war in which millions of men are killed,' he was saying. 'What can it matter to some poor booby who runs away whether he's shot at by a firing squad or whether he's shoved back in the line to be shot at by the enemy?'

He looked round his listeners and was surprised to find his half-flippant remark not taken up in similar vein. Everyone suddenly looked grim – even the butler and footman, standing side by side against the wall, not listening but unable not to hear.

Then Virginia said quietly, 'My son was Court Martialled for cowardice in the field, and found guilty. At his own request he was sent back into action and was killed. I'm sure it mattered a great deal to him how he was killed. It did to me.'

The silence after she had spoken hung in the air for almost a minute. Sir Guy Paynter's face registered horror, but his feeling was one of annoyance. A man who took supercilious delight from other people's *gaffes*, he prided himself on never making one. Before accepting the hospitality of comparative strangers he made a point of reading them up in the appropriate social registers and inquiring about them of his friends. He had been able to find out little about Virginia Bellamy, because of her undistinguished provincial background, and it had never occurred to Polly Merivale to tell him of the wartime tragedy. In fact, he realised as he glanced at Polly now, she was rather enjoying his discomfiture over it.

He got to his feet and said quietly to Virginia, 'I am so sorry. Of course, I had no idea that you were personally involved in the question.'

She was too deeply hurt to return a conventional acceptance of the apology.

'Even if I weren't,' she snapped, 'I hope I would have the sensitivity to feel for those who were.'

He bowed slightly.

'I stand corrected. I'd better be off before I disgrace myself completely. Polly, can I give you a lift, or are you going to stay and have your character improved?'

'Oh, you know my character is beyond praying for, let alone improving.'

She rose as he bowed again to Virginia, thanked her for a most delicious luncheon, and bade farewell to everyone in turn. Then he ushered Polly to the door, opened by Hudson, and followed her out.

Later, when Lady Prue had gone and James had retired to his room to play his gramophone, Virginia told Richard, 'I'm awfully sorry about what happened.'

'I can quite understand your being upset, my dear. It's just a pity you couldn't have accepted his apology when he made it.'

'I didn't believe he really meant it. Besides, it annoyed me that he obviously thinks he's so rich he can say anything he likes and people will put up with it. I hate to think of a man like that having influence.'

'You mean, you hate to think that I'm prepared to make use of it.' Well, I can assure you, Virginia, things are always done this way – a word here, a word there, a little discreet string-pulling. They have always been done that way in politics of all parties, and I'm sure they always will be.'

'Then I think it's a great pity.'

Her stubborn refusal to appreciate the situation irritated him suddenly. He said sourly, 'Anyway, the whole thing was my fault for asking you to give the luncheon in the first place. I know you don't want to be a political hostess.'

'Like Marjorie,' she couldn't prevent herself flashing back.

The sharp little tiff was interrupted by the entry of Hudson, bearing a wrapped bunch of roses.

'For you, m'lady. Delivered by hand just now.'

He handed them to Virginia and retired. She fished out the accompanying card.

' "Please forgive me. I am proud to believe that my own mother would defend her son as you defended yours. Guy Paynter." '

'They're beautiful,' she had to admit, burying her nose in one of the rich blooms.

Richard was smiling when she looked up.

Virginia was able to thank the sender personally next morning. Just as she was writing a note to him he was announced by Hudson.

'I really came,' he said, after thanks and mutual apologies had been expressed, 'to see whether by any extraordinary chance you were free to come and have lunch at the Ritz. Arnold Bennett is coming.'

'Oh, I've always wanted to meet him!'

'And Freddie Birkenhead. And a rather interesting young musician. Malcolm Sargent.'

It was irresistible and she was free. It was her ideal chance to make it up to Richard, to Paynter, and to herself.

'What time were you . . . ?'

'We've arranged to meet in the Long Bar of the Trocadero first for a cocktail. So if you really would do us the honour of joining us, we could go there in my car now.'

'Oh, I'd have to change.'

He smiled. 'Naturally. By "now" I meant in the hour or so that any woman takes to change from one frock into another and to comb her hair.'

Virginia laughed. 'I'm glad you understand these things. But what will you do while I'm gone?'

'Stay here and make myself at home. There's a lot to be learned from someone's room.'

'And what do you learn from this one so far?'

He glanced round it.

'That you have good taste without ostentation. Family affection without being a *hausfrau*. Elegance without snobbery.'

'I'm sure that's flattery – but I must admit I enjoy it.'

'Now, why are pleasant things always called flattery and ugly things called the truth? Dear Lady Bellamy – Virginia, if I may? – do let us admit the truth to each other, however pleasant it may be.'

They exchanged warm smiles and Virginia went away to change, leaving her intriguing flatterer to wander round the room, peering at every picture and ornament with a discerning eye. She was back with him in under half the hour.

'I don't like it,' Mrs. Bridges was saying. 'In my young days we went out with the milkman or the postman or the butcher's boy . . .' Or a policeman, she recalled with momentary wistfulness from the depths of personal memory, but did not say it. 'Anyway, someone respectable,' she concluded instead.

'He may be respectable, Mrs. Bridges,' Daisy said.

'A man that answers advertisements? I'd never trust a man like that.'

'I really think you should have stopped her, Rose,' Mr. Hudson said. 'To engage in correspondence might have improved even Ruby's mind. But to allow her to go and meet a man who is, in effect, a total stranger . . .'

For Ruby was the one person absent from the servants' hall that evening. In her best hat and coat, and a deal too much powder and lipstick, she had gone to her first encounter with the quietly disposed Mr. Herbert Turner. It was ten o'clock now, and she had not returned.

'I couldn't stop her,' Rose protested.

'She's over twenty-one,' Edward pointed out.

Daisy giggled. 'You don't think he wants her for the white slave trade, Mr. Hudson?'

The others' expression registered the unlikelihood of the proposition. Only Mr. Hudson still showed genuine concern.

'She is not . . . well, versed in the ways of the world,' he answered gravely.

At that moment the area door was heard to open and shut. Frederick looked at his watch as relief showed all round. A moment later, Ruby appeared in the doorway, beaming idiotically.

'Ruby, you are late.'

'Sorry, Mr. Hudson.'

Mrs. Bridges snorted. 'How dare you go out and meet someone without telling me?'

'Yes, Mrs. Bridges.'

Ruby turned to depart, thereby disappointing them all. Daisy asked quickly, on the general behalf: 'What was he like, Ruby?'

The girl turned back again.

'Oh, he was ever so nice.'

'Stood you a bit of supper after the pictures, did he?' Frederick deduced.

'Oh, yes. I had tomato fish-cakes and bread and butter, and an ice cream and a nice pot of tea.'

She yawned suddenly.

'I must go to bed now. Goodnight, Mrs. Bridges. Goodnight, Mr. Hudson.'

Daisy and Edward went off to their own apartment over the garage and Frederick to his room. The butler and the cook sat on, silent and ruminative, for some minutes.

'We cannot stop the girl going out,' Hudson said at length. 'She has the right to meet whom she pleases, so long as she does not bring him back here.'

Mrs. Bridges' eyes gleamed with sudden inspiration.

'That's just what I want her to do, Mr. Hudson. Bring him back here. I feel responsible for that girl, and I reckon it's my duty at least to find out what sort of man he is. Yes, that's what we'll do, if you agree, Angus – have him to Sunday tea, and take a good look at him.'

Hudson, who preferred life to remain above all things orderly and free from nagging little irritations and worries, supported the idea readily, and the following morning, when the breakfast bustle was over, Ruby received her orders.

Three days later, in the afternoon, the denizens of Downstairs awaited Herbert Turner's coming with mixed expectations. Despite her reservations, Mrs. Bridges had given him the benefit of the doubt by changing out of her working clothes into one of her best dresses and had chivvied the others into laying the servants' hall table with tea things as correctly as if the guest they were about to receive for scrutiny was worthy of established respect. And, indeed, they were agreeably relieved when at last there came the knock at the door and Ruby, wearing her best green dress and, with her hair carefully done and not wearing her spectacles, looking passably attractive for once in her life, went out and in a few moments returned with a neatly dressed man with short-back-and-sides haircut and small round spectacles. He paused to stand self-consciously just inside the room.

Blushing faintly through the thickness of face powder, Ruby announced, 'This is Mr. Herbert Turner. Mrs. Bridges, Mr. Hudson, Miss Buck, Mrs. Barnes, Mr. Norton, Mr. Barnes.'

'Very pleased to make your acquaintance,' Mr. Turner said as his first utterance, bobbing his head in a little gesture of respect. His speech was precise and 'clerkly'. 'It's very kind of you to invite me here, I'm sure.'

'A pleasure, Mr. Turner,' Mrs. Bridges beamed; and Mr. Hudson hastened to indicate a chair at the table and say, 'Won't you sit down here, Mr. Turner? I imagine tea is ready, Mrs. Bridges?'

'Quite ready, Mr. Hudson. Ruby, you sit down, too. Daisy, perhaps you'd be so kind as to fetch the tea?'

Daisy had not foreseen this development and wasn't too sure that she approved of it; but there was no refusing, so she went off into the kitchen with her nose a little higher in the air than usual.

'You live in Balham, I believe, Mr. Turner?' Mrs. Bridges was saying.

'Yes. My parents and I have a house there.'

'A very pleasant area,' Mr. Hudson said.

'Oh, yes. Unfortunately, my mother is a martyr to rheumatism and my father's health has not been good since he was gassed in the war.'

'In the trenches, was he?' Edward asked, more interested now.

'Yes, Mr. Barnes. He was one of the Old Contemptibles.'

'Was you in the army, then?' asked the other ex-Serviceman, Frederick.

Their guest shook his head and glanced around them uncertainly.

'I'm afraid not. I always feel very awkward about it because, well, I was kept out by . . . by flat feet, of all things. Of course, being in the Post Office I was considered to be in a reserved occupation, but naturally I volunteered, and that was the answer I got.'

'Well,' Mr. Hudson said, trying to spare the man's feelings, ' "They also serve who only stand and wait".'

'Even with flat feet?' responded their guest, and got a general laugh which eased the tension immediately.

Indeed, as tea progressed Mr. Turner revealed himself to be the possessor of quite a pawky vein of humour and a lively interest in everyday matters which coincided to an agreeable extent with that of his hosts. The chance mention of the latest murder sensation in Sussex provoked an animated discussion in which he argued freely with Edward and Frederick until, upon the introduction of some of the more gruesome particulars, Mrs. Bridges called for an end to the subject.

'My fault entirely, Mrs. Bridges,' Mr. Turner apologised. 'I mentioned it first. I'm sure I did.'

'Are you interested in crime?' Hudson asked, trying to restore the guest's ease.

'Well, I think we all are a bit, Mr. Hudson, don't you? It's the drama of it, I always think. But I prefer what one might call a better class of murder. The classic cases, you know.'

'Fancy that!' Mrs. Bridges declared, admiring a scholar, and pressed Mr. Turner to another generous slice of her specially baked cake. Without perhaps realising it, they were all beginning to feel he was one of them already.

Carrying crockery into the kitchen together when the meal was over, Edward murmured to his wife, 'What d'you think?'

Daisy answered, 'I don't know what he sees in *her*.'

Overhearing, Frederick said, 'Ruby hasn't hardly said a word since he's been here. You know what I think? I reckon he's grateful to have a found a good listener.'

Ruby had gone up to her room to apply yet more powder and get into her outdoor clothes. With the other servants busy, Mr. Hudson and Mrs. Bridges were left alone with Herbert Turner for a few minutes. They proceeded to interrogate him in a way more suited to Ruby's parents than to her superiors in service.

'How old are you, Mr. Turner, if I might ask?'

'Thirty-five, Mr. Hudson, And done nothing, as you might say. I've lived a very quiet life, what with the war and my parents being invalids. Too quiet, really. I read the novels of H. G. Wells, and about those people he writes about who just . . . well, just exist. And I think, well, that's me.'

Mrs. Bridges asked carefully, 'Haven't you thought of getting married ever?'

'Well, I have, Mrs. Bridges, but I'm afraid money's always been a bit tight. Until my recent promotion, that is.'

He glanced from one to the other, swallowed visibly,

and added, 'I . . . I suppose I may as well admit that's why I answered that advertisement.'

Mr. Hudson was on the point of eliciting further details of Mr. Turner's hopes and intentions, but Ruby robbed him of the chance by entering in coat and hat. Mr. Turner rose with the alacrity of relief.

'Ah, there she is. Well, we'll be off, if you'll excuse us. I thought we might go back for a bite of supper with my parents a bit later.'

Mrs. Bridges stood up. 'Well, all right, Mr. Turner. But I don't want her home late, if you please.'

'Oh, no, Mrs. Bridges, I wouldn't do that. She's a bit too . . . precious for that.'

The simper on Ruby's vivid scarlet mouth was almost nauseating.

'All right, Ruby?' he asked, offering his arm.

'Yes . . . Herbert.'

The farewells to Mr. Hudson, Mrs. Bridges and the rest were mutually warm. Mr. Herbert Turner had been tested and approved.

'Well, Mrs. Bridges,' Hudson said, 'I think you can start looking for a new kitchen-maid.'

When Daisy opined that anyone who would want to go out with Ruby must be 'a proper Charlie', both rebuked her.

Virginia had completely forgiven Guy Paynter's indiscretion to the extent of having forgotten that he had ever uttered it. She had enjoyed the luncheon at the Ritz immensely. As the only woman present, she had been the centre of attention from the susceptible Arnold Bennett, who had stammered compliments. The ebullient Lord Birkenhead had coruscated especially for her with the witty erudition which few men of the time could match. Young Malcolm Sargent had proved intelligent and gallant in a way which Virginia sensed would be difficult for any woman to resist in years to come. Guy had been amusing, scandalously gossipy, and most assiduously attentive to her. The food and wines he had chosen quite outdid anything she was accustomed to.

'Why not?' Richard said later. He and James had been listening to her account of the occasion and he had raised his eyebrows and smiled when she added, a little diffidently, that Guy had invited her to lend him her support a fortnight hence at his country house, Shelbourne, where he was giving one of his celebrated 'political weekends'.

'You don't mind, then?'

'My dear, I'm only too delighted. I'd hate you to miss such a chance.'

'Won't it look rather strange, though – if I'm there without you?'

'Just because I have to go to Paris to meet the French Foreign Minister is no reason for your refusing a pleasant invitation while I'm away. People understand these things nowadays.'

'I suppose so. He sent me this round.'

She held up a small book.

'What is it?'

'Browning's poems. An autographed first edition.'

James whistled. 'That must be worth a pretty penny.'

'I know. We were talking about first editions, and which ones we'd particularly like to possess. I said I'd like to have a favourite book of poems, so that every time I read it I could pretend it was sent to me personally by the author. Perhaps I should take it back when I go to Shelbourne.'

She went out. The note which had accompanied the gift lay on the table beside James. Without stooping he could read the flamboyant scrawl: 'Just to thank you for being such a perfect hostess.'

'Father,' he said, 'do you think it's a good thing, Virginia seeing so much of Paynter?'

Richard regarded his son for a few moments before replying, 'She's perfectly safe with him.'

'Why do you say that?'

'For a reason I could not possibly mention to her.'

'You don't mean he's married?'

'No. He is ... not the marrying sort.'

Understanding dawned on James's face. Richard continued, 'He's devoted to his mother. Innumerable ladies have acted as hostess at his table, and I dare say at least half of them expected to marry him. I'm sure nothing would horrify him more than to have a woman permanently in his house – or even temporarily in his bed.'

'Well, I'm damned!'

'Fortunately, Virginia is much too innocent to understand these things. I'm only too happy for her to enjoy herself with what one might reasonably describe as a safe man. She'll have a wonderful weekend.'

She did, too. With Rose to attend her whenever she needed a change, a bath, or a refurbishment of her make-up, and to supply a familiar presence in unfamiliar surroundings, Virginia revelled in meeting the distinguished, the ultra-fashionable, above all the scintillating, men and women whom Guy Paynter habitually selected as his guests. Her quiet intelligence and unostentatious beauty charmed them in turn, and the regretful farewells when the last taxi-load departed on the Sunday evening were as sincere as they were prolonged.

Guy led Virginia back into the drawing-room of his superbly furnished manor house, with its quiet lighting, *trompe l'oeuil* impression of classical columns and arches and paved pathway, and steadily burning open fire in a large hearth.

'Why do one's guests always have to take forty minutes to say goodbye?' he groaned, stretching. 'Parsons, we'll have a bottle of champagne, please. And some caviare. Not that horrid black stuff. Haven't we some of the amber?'

'Yes, sir,' his butler said, and went out.

'I'm sure they'll miss the train and all arrive back here insisting on staying the night,' Guy continued to Virginia, leaning in mock dejection against the mantelpiece. 'I must say I hope they don't, especially Margot. One never knows the meaning of a long weekend until one has Margot to stay.'

Virginia laughed. 'You know you enjoyed every minute of it.'

'No. I did *not* enjoy Winston's rendering of "My Old Dutch". As for Lloyd George's Welsh hymns, I've never admired them as much as many people pretend to.'

'But *they* enjoyed it. That was the important thing. The whole weekend has been a great success.'

He straightened up and went to kiss her gently on the cheek.

'Thanks to you. You are a splendid hostess.'

'No, I just like people.'

'And they like you. Now then, I thought you might like to see Charlie Chaplin's new film. I managed to get hold of a copy.'

'*The Gold Rush!* You . . . don't mean to say you have a private cinema here?'

'I don't usually tell people, or they want to spend the entire weekend watching Felix the Cat or Harold Lloyd when I want to play bridge. But as it's just the two of us I thought it might amuse you.'

'Yes.' Virginia hesitated. 'I didn't realise we were . . . going to be alone here tonight.'

'Does it embarrass you?'

'It does, rather.'

He laughed out loud.

'The thing I love about you is your delicious honesty. My mother would adore you. I say, would you come to a little dinner at her house? Tuesday?'

'I'd love to meet her, but Richard gets back tomorrow and I'm not sure what he's doing.'

'Not Richard. D'you mind? Just you. She's a little bit of an invalid and doesn't go about much. But a quiet dinner party, with just one person . . .'

Virginia was regarding him calculatingly as he gazed seemingly pleadingly into her eyes. The return of the butler interrupted what he was saying. Champagne in an ice bucket, an opened pot of caviare, biscuits and the appropriate impedimenta were set down.

'All right, Parsons,' Guy said. 'I'll deal with it.'

The man bowed and went out. Paynter went to draw the champagne cork.

'I wonder how Richard's getting on?' Virginia said deliberately. 'It's a very important meeting. He does care so much. I . . . I wish he could get a post in the Government again – where he could put his talents to better use.'

Guy's back was half to her as he worked gently at the cork. He was smiling to himself.

'Yes. Of course, it's not so easy, now he's in the Lords.'

Virginia faltered on, 'I believe there's . . . a post of . . . of Under-Secretary of State for Foreign Affairs which is going to be vacant. It would be rather nice if . . .'

The cork came out of the bottle with a cultured sigh. Guy poured two glasses and brought her one.

'You know,' he said, 'I would do anything to please you. If I happen to have any influence in that direction I will certainly use it.'

They raised their glasses to touch gently and sipped a little. Then he wandered away to cover some of the biscuits with caviare. Virginia watched him uneasily, wishing she hadn't spoken. It was too late.

'You know,' he was saying over his shoulder, 'I thought of taking my yacht on a long cruise this summer. I was talking to the Prince of Wales last week. I think he'll probably come, and Freddie Birkenhead and one or two others. It just occurs to me . . . I wonder if you'd like to come. Richard could join us, whenever his duties allow.'

He returned with the plate of generously covered biscuits, and a napkin, which he set on a small table beside the settee.

'Well, Virginia? What do you say?'

She found herself looking up at him, wondering, unable to answer. Suddenly, she wished she was back in Eaton Place – or even upstairs, in some small room where the familiar, dependable Rose was probably reading her magazine tales of romantic make-believe.

'You know, Daisy,' said Rose next evening, 'I never saw such luxury in my life. They even had champagne in the servants' hall.'

She dumped Virginia's empty luggage on the table.

'Sounds a bit of all right to me,' Edward said, as he examined them. 'I'll give these a bit of a rub up before they're put away.'

'Ta, Eddie. Mind, it wasn't as good the last night, after all the others had gone.'

'All gone, Rose?' The inquiry came from Mr. Hudson, who had emerged from his pantry just in time to overhear. 'You mean, her ladyship stayed on alone last evening?'

Rose stared back at him, her mind working upon implications which had not so far occurred to her. The others watched her silently. After some moments, Ruby, who had been fidgeting in the background, spoke up.

'Mrs. Bridges, can I have tonight off, instead of next week? Herbert can't get off next week. It's his turn to be on duty in the evenings.'

'Oh, very well,' Mrs. Bridges snapped, her mind concerned with greater issues. 'Only, don't make a habit of it. Now, come on, Rose. Lunch is waiting. It'll all get cold.'

The servants sat down to table in preoccupied mood, though none more so than Rose.

'Well?' Polly Merivale asked James. 'Did your stepmother enjoy her weekend at Shelbourne?'

'Very much, I believe. Weren't you there?'

'Oh, no. "The Queen is dead; long live the Queen".'

He scowled. 'I don't think that's very funny.'

'Nor do I.' She wandered away to the morning-room mirror, to adjust her hat. 'Do you know where she's going tonight?'

'No.'

'She is going to dine with Guy's mother. I wonder if your father knows?'

'I imagine so,' James said, controlling his temper with no little difficulty.

Mrs. Merivale turned and came back to him.

'I wonder if he really *knows*?' she said, and he frowned less with anger than with curiosity. 'I nearly got invited there, James. Just before I came here to lunch with Guy that day. I knew at once what it meant. It meant that, after years of fending off every woman in sight like a demented old ocean-going tug, his dear mama had said "Guy, dear, you must get married. You know you'll need someone to look after you when I'm gone".'

James grinned at last. This woman really was a bitch.

'Sit down and stop talking rubbish, Polly,' he ordered. 'Look, I'm sorry if you're upset because your friendship with Guy has broken up, but that's no reason to . . .'

'You know why it did?' she interrupted, smiling in return. 'I cared too much. Oh, not for Guy. I don't like charm and ruthlessness in men. One or the other, but not both together.'

'Then, if you felt like that . . .'

'All that money, James. It's so beastly being poor. Harry left a mass of debts, and all I have is my widow's pension and a pittance his parents give me. Then along comes Guy, and suddenly I've only to mention something and have it. To say "I'd like to go to New York", and you're there. "Wouldn't it be pleasant to cruise round the Mediterranean" – and it happened. It's irresistible – or almost. I'm sure Lady Bellamy will find it so.'

She flashed him her brightest smile and went swiftly, leaving him staring.

'Father,' he said late that evening.

'Mm?'

Richard had not long returned from the Lords. Virginia had been out since before lunch and had still not come in.

'Has . . . Virginia said anything about . . . about Paynter lately?'

Richard looked surprised. 'Of course, from time to time. She's out with him and some others today. Brighton or somewhere. He has a new Lagonda he wanted to show off.'

'I . . . see.'

'As a matter of fact, he's invited her on his yacht in the summer. I shall join them, as and when.'

'Oh, no!'

'What on earth does that mean?'

'Father, you must forbid her to see him.'

'Forbid!' To James's irritation his father was actually smiling. 'I hardly think I can do that. And I'm very sure Virginia wouldn't obey me if I did. Besides . . .' He hesitated momentarily, 'If you must know, it was I who first asked her to cultivate his acquaintance. I wanted him to use his influence to get me a post.'

'Oh, for God's sake, Father! Do you mean to say that some post means more to you than Virginia does?'

Richard suddenly raged back, 'How dare you say that? Of course it doesn't! I've already told you, haven't I, that Virginia's perfectly safe with Guy Paynter? As safe as that Polly Merivale or any of the others have been. She's enjoying his company, and I'm glad for her, and that's all there is to it. Really, James, I do wish you would stop your eternal interfering in other people's happiness.'

James's face muscles twitched.

'There is such a thing as respect,' he retorted. 'Does anyone respect Polly Merivale and the others? Will they respect Virginia – or you, when it gets about that you bought some job or other with her reputation? Don't you understand that, Father? Or don't you care?'

He crashed out of the room, leaving Richard to sink into a fireside chair and stare into the glowing coals, suddenly horrified by the images he could picture there.

He was sitting there when Virginia came in. She wore a loose pink coat over a white dress and carried a white hat in one hand, her handbag and gloves in the other. A single strand of pearls was about her throat.

'Still up, Richard?' she said. 'I'm sorry I'm so late. We had dinner at Brighton.'

'You and Guy?' he asked, still picturing things in the fire.

'And the rest. Is . . . anything wrong?'

He got up stiffly and faced her.

'Virginia, I want to ask you something. You remember I asked you a favour a short time ago. I want to ask you a much greater one now. I want to ask you not to see so much of Guy Paynter.'

'You mean, you've got the Under-Secretaryship now?' she said it without sarcasm.

'No. That's nothing to do with it. You know, I've been made to feel my age quite often, lately . . . but I find suddenly that I'm still young enough to be jealous.'

The merest fraction of time elapsed before she flung her arms round his neck and pressed her cheek against his.

'Oh, Richard! I'm so glad!'

At that very moment, Ruby was facing an outraged Mrs. Bridges in the servants' hall. Mr. Hudson and Rose looked on.

'I've told you twice already, my girl, I will not have you stopping out this late, Herbert Turner or no Herbert Turner. I spoke to him when he first came here, and he agreed. I'm as disappointed in him as in you.'

'Yes, Mrs. Bridges.'

'It's not respectable in a young girl. Besides, you're only half awake in the mornings as it is, without late gallivanting.'

'It won't happen again, Mrs. Bridges.'

'It certainly won't. I'll see to that. You'll fetch that Herbert Turner round here and I'll have a few words to say to him, too.'

Rose ventured to ask kindly, 'Did you have a nice evening, Ruby?'

'Oh, yes.'

'I mean, did he . . . have anything special to say, like?'

'Oh, yes. He asked me to marry him.'

'Marry!' Mrs. Bridges almost shrieked. 'Well, why didn't you say, girl?'

'Because I said I wasn't interested, Mrs. Bridges.'

'You said *what*?'

'I thanked him very much for the honour, but I wasn't interested.'

Three stunned expressions faced her. She explained patiently, 'He was all right, but he hadn't got much go in him, really. Besides, he would never give up his father and 'specially his mother, and I didn't want to spend my days as nursemaid to invalids while he'd be out to his work.'

'*And*,' she closed the subject, once and for all, 'he didn't look nothing like his photograph. He wasn't a bit like Rudolph Valentino.'

Next afternoon, Sir Guy Paynter was shown into the morning-room, where Virginia and James sat. He was, as always, immaculately dressed, with a fresh buttonhole. The bland smile was on his lips as he nodded a silent greeting to James.

'Thank you for your note,' he said to Virginia. 'It was kind of you to send it round by hand, so that I should receive it as soon as possible.'

Virginia moistened her lips and explained to James, 'I had to refuse Guy's kind invitation to go on his yacht this summer. Richard and I are going to Austria.'

Guy said, 'Actually, I really just came round to pick up the book I lent you.'

'Book?'

'Browning's poems.' He glanced at the desk on which the little volume lay.

'Ah, of course,' Virginia smiled, and brought it to him. 'Thank you for lending it to me.'

'Not at all. Goodbye, Virginia. Goodbye, Major Bellamy.'

Still smiling, he bowed and showed himself out of the room.

'Well!' James exclaimed. 'Pretty cheap of him to take the book back.'

'Yes, I thought so. But effeminate men often are rather petty.'

'Effem . . . ! Does . . . does Father know you know?'

'Oh, no. He'd be terribly embarrassed. James, please – I'd rather he didn't.'

James gave her a reassuring grin, but said nothing.

They were still together when Richard came in a quarter of an hour later.

'Well?' Virginia asked. 'What did Mr. Baldwin want?'

'He sent for me to offer me the post of Under-Secretary of State for Foreign Affairs.'

James moved quickly to this father and shook his hand.

'Well done, Father. I hoped you'd get it.'

Virginia was looking puzzled.

'You don't mean . . . that Guy . . . ?'

'Sir Guy Paynter had been round and left a note at Downing Street earlier this morning. For some reason it had occurred to him suddenly to advise the Prime Minister that I was much too old to return to the Government.'

Virginia's hands flew to her mouth, but Richard was going on, smiling into her widened eyes.

'Baldwin said that that had made up his mind. He said he'd always considered giving the post to me, but he didn't want to have someone who appeared to be in Guy Paynter's pocket.'

He and Virginia regarded one another solemnly for some seconds. Then she was in his arms again and James was making a quiet exit, to go up to his room and put on his gramophone a record which caused the servants who heard it to raise their heads in surprise at its unusual cheerfulness.

The Upstairs, Downstairs Series from Sphere:

Adventure Fiction from Sphere:

Historical Romance from Sphere:

All Sphere Books are available at your bookshop or newsagent, or can be ordered from the following address: Sphere Books, Cash Sales Department, P.O. Box 11, Falmouth, Cornwall.

Please send cheque or postal order (no currency), and allow 18p for postage and packing for the first book plus 8p per copy for each additional book ordered up to a maximum charge of 66p in U.K.

Customers in Eire and B.F.P.O. please allow 18p for postage and packing for the first book plus 8p per copy for the next 6 books, thereafter 3p per book.

Overseas customers please allow 20p for postage and packing for the first book and 10p per copy for each additional book.